Shawty Down To Ride For

A Boss

Tina J

Copyright 2019

Warning:

This book is strictly Urban Fiction and the story is **NOT**

REAL!

Characters will not behave the way you want them to; nor will

they react to situations the way you think they should. Some of

them may be drug addicts, kingpins, savages, thugs, rich, poor,

ho's, sluts, haters, bitter ex-girlfriends or boyfriends, people

from the past and the list can go on and on. That is what Urban

Fiction mostly consists of. If this isn't anything you foresee

yourself interested in, then do yourself a favor and don't read it

because it's only going to piss you off.

Also, the book will not end the way you want so please be

advised that the outcome will be based solely on my own

thoughts and ideas. Thanks so much to my readers, supporters,

publisher and fellow authors and authoress for the support.

Author Tina J

More books from me:

The Thug I Chose 1, 2 & 3

A Thin Line Between Me and My Thug 1 & 2

I Got Luv For My Shawty 1 & 2

Kharis and Caleb: A Different Kind of Love 1 & 2

Loving You Is A Battle 1 & 2 & 3

Violet and The Connect 1 & 2 & 3

You Complete Me

Love Will Lead You Back

This Thing Called Love

Are We In This Together 1,2 &3

Shawty Down To Ride For a Boss 1, 2 &3

When A Boss Falls in Love 1, 2 & 3

Let Me Be The One 1 & 2

We Got That Forever Love

Aint No Savage Like The One I Got 1&2

A Queen and A Hustla 1, 2 & 3

Thirsty For A Bad Boy 1&2

Hassan and Serena: An Unforgettable Love 1&2

Caught Up Loving A Beast 1, 2 & 3

A Street King And His Shawty 1 & 2

I Fell For The Wrong Bad Boy 1&2

I Wanna Love You 1 & 2

Addicted to Loving a Boss 1, 2, & 3

I Need That Gangsta Love 1&2

Creepin With The Plug 1 & 2

All Eyes On The Crown 1,2&3

When She's Bad, I'm Badder: Jiao and Dreek, A Crazy

Love Story 1,2&3

Still Luvin A Beast 1&2

Her Man, His Savage 1 & 2

Marco & Rakia: Not Your Ordinary, Hood Kinda Love 1,2

& 3

Feenin For A Real One 1, 2 & 3

A Kingpin's Dynasty 1, 2 & 3

What Kinda Love Is This: Captivating A Boss 1, 2 & 3

Frankie & Lexi: Luvin A Young Beast 1, 2 & 3

A Dope Boys Seduction 1, 2 & 3

My Brother's Keeper 1. 2 & 3

C'Yani & Meek: A Dangerous Hood Love 1, 2 & 3

When A Savage Falls for A Good Girl 1, 2 & 3

Eva & Deray 1 & 2

Blame It On His Gangsta Luv 1 & 2

Falling for The Wrong Hustla 1, 2 & 3

I Gave My Heart to A Jersey Killa 1, 2 & 3

Luvin The Son of a Savage 1, 2 & 3

A Dopeman and His Shawty 1, 2 & 3

Somebody Else's Thug 1, 2 & 3

Steel (Akeem)

Me and my brother Aiden were sitting in McDonald's eating with a few of our soldiers when two dudes came in to rob the place. This was the type of fuckery I didn't tolerate. There were too many innocent people in harm's way. And for what? I mean how much money did they think was coming out of here? I put my burger down, took a sip of my soda and headed in the direction of the stupid ass niggas that assumed this was a good idea.

The first one to stand up behind me was my brother and then everyone else followed suit. He and I were like one and the same. I was more the calm one and he was the hotheaded one that killed first and still didn't ask questions later. Aiden and I had the same mom but different fathers, but that didn't mean a damn thing to us. The bottom line was we both came from my mothers' pussy and that's all that mattered.

"Yo what the fuck you doing?" I barked out at them and one of them dropped their gun.

"That's the stupid shit I be talking about. How you rob a place and then drop the weapon?" Aiden said, leaning on the counter.

"Oh shit Steel, I didn't know you were in here."

"It shouldn't matter if I am or not. Who the hell robs a McDonald's?"

"Did you give them any money?" I asked the cashier who had tears running down her face, probably from being

7

scared.

"No."

"Get the fuck out of here." I told them and they hauled ass.

I nodded my head to my soldiers and they knew what to do without me speaking a word. They knew what to do and I'm sure I would receive the call later. My brother and I walked back and tossed our food.

"Let's get the hell out of here. I lost my fucking appetite."

Aiden was behind me and hopped in my brand new Phantom with me. We rode to my mom and pop's house because she had been blowing both of us up saying she needed to talk to us about something. We walked in the house and I saw her and Block sitting in the kitchen. He had his arms wrapped around her waist whispering something in her ear, making her smile. That's the type of love I couldn't wait to experience. I thought I had that with Farrah, but the bitch turned out to be crazier than I knew. The best thing out of our relationship was my three-year-old daughter. But that's for another time.

Aiden's father was the one who helped her raise me and was still with my mom to this day. He was a retired OG that ran a drug empire with an iron fist that he entrusted to both of us about six years ago, and we run it the same way. My dad wasn't shit and I was never ashamed to admit it.

My father ran the drug empire in Africa. Yes, I had African in my blood. He was the dad that cheated on his main chick for the side chick. Then he got the side chick pregnant and she decided to keep it; only the kid had to remain a secret as well. Yeah, my dad sent my mom hefty checks and we didn't want for anything. My mom never spent those checks and kept them in an account for me. She didn't want to spend any of his guilt money and my pops kept her laced with everything she and I needed anyway.

Yeah, I considered Aiden's dad mine as well. Between that money and what Aiden's dad hooked us up with, he and I were multi-millionaires. We were well respected and feared over here on the entire East Coast. Niggas knew not to try us and many lost their lives trying.

"Honey can you step in the living room for a minute," My mom asked when she saw us walk in. I knew some shit was about to go down if she needed to talk to me. I stepped inside and was greeted by my punk ass dad and a few other people.

"Hello, son."

"Son. Man go 'head with that shit. I haven't seen your ass since I was born and now I'm your son. Nigga please. You can address me as Akeem just like anyone else I just met."

He stood up and walked over to me, looked me up and down and gave me a rib shot. I found the shit funny because it showed me that he was threatened. After I caught my breath, I

9

hit him with a two-piece and followed it up with a few rib shots. His security immediately sprang into action trying to break it up. Aiden was right there next to me, fucking up some of his men. When Block came to see what was going on, it was as if everyone stopped. My pops Block had shit on lock. Whether he was out the game or not, he was still well respected and he didn't play when it came to my mom or his two sons.

"Ok, now that that's out of the way, can we sit down and act like adults? My mom said rolling her eyes.

"What the fuck does his punk ass want?"

I was beyond mad and they wanted me to sit here to listen to his bullshit. He went on and on about the nigga Miguel from Puerto Rico that was their Connect and had killed both of his sons over his wife. They must've done some deep shit to her for him to kill them. I had no remorse for them. Brother or not, I didn't know them and everyone knows you don't fuck with a man's wife; that's just common sense. Little did he know, Miguel was our Connect and we rocked with him, so if he was looking for beef with him, he could leave now. The one thing Block taught us was to always stay loyal and you will never be tested.

After the loser sperm donor finished talking, I learned these brothers of mine crossed so many people that I may need more people to guard us.

"Look, we good over here as far as working. I don't

need to go to Africa to do that. However, my brother and I will take a trip out there to see what type of operation you got running. I'll put some things in place and then we're bringing our asses back."

"Your brother?"

"Yes, my brother. You would know I had one if you stayed in touch. It's all good though, my pops had my back and always will."

Block nodded and I think it pissed the sperm donor off, but who gave a fuck about how he was feeling.

"I'll be in touch," he said walking out.

This nigga had the nerve to look my mom up and down and lick his lips. She sucked her teeth and rolled her eyes. Block must've missed it because he damn sure would've said something. He was crazy in love with my mom. He didn't even want the people at the store to tell her to have a good day.

"No need. If I need you, I'll hit your line."

After they left, I dropped Aiden off at his house and drove over to my mini-mansion. I put the key in my lock and Brea greeted me at the door with her smile. My ex was still staying in this house and I was cool with that. I had a new one being built. Brea followed me around the house until it was time for her to go to bed. Unfortunately, her mother did the same thing.

Farrah was kind of my high school sweetheart, but not really. I met her in the middle of my senior year. She was a sophomore and new to the school. She and I met, clicked, and were together ever since. I was her first everything from what she tells me and when we had our first sexual experience, I knew I was.

Farrah was a beautiful woman. She was five-foot-six, if that, with creamy milk chocolate skin. She had an ok body, but over the years she stayed in the gym and hired a personal trainer to get one of the video vixen bodies. Yes, she was smart and could hold decent conversations, but once she graduated high school all her dreams and goals went out the window. All she wanted to do was shop and go on vacations. I didn't have a problem because it ain't tricking if you got it, but after a while it started to turn me off.

I broke up with her almost a year ago, but for some reason she's still around and not just for my daughter. I'm partly to blame because one, I could've moved out a long time ago and two, if she was offering the pussy, a nigga was taking it. Sadly, she assumed that would keep me around, but it didn't do anything but prove that she would do anything to keep me. Farrah was fully aware of all the women I kept, but stayed around anyway. I couldn't be with a woman who was ok with that. To each his own, but that just wasn't me.

Now we're sitting here, having the same conversation about me going out and not wanting her. I could see now that she was going to be a problem if and when I chose to be with someone else. I just hoped if I was feeling the woman, she didn't get distracted and say fuck it. A nigga like me was ready to settle down and find that woman I could marry and have a family with. Yea, sleeping with different women was fun but it got tiring.

Farrah

Yes, I'm Akeem's baby mother from hell, let him tell it. The only problem is I'm not and he needs to stop telling people that. So what if I black out when he walks in when the sun is coming up, or the fact that I've been fighting chicks over them calling my phone telling me how good his dick is. The list goes on and on when it comes to dealing with a BOSS like Akeem. Yes, my daughter's father was what women fantasize about having lie next to them every night. But shit ain't always peaches and cream when you fucking with someone like him. Yes, the sex is all that, but the bullshit that comes along with it isn't worth it.

I had everything I needed, except for the love I wanted. I'm sure he loved me at one point but the way he'd been acting lately, showed me that Steel fell out of love with me. However, I am still very much in love with him. My daughter is what keeps him here and I'm sure that will change soon.

Akeem and Aiden are what the world sees as a BOSS. They were beyond rich, smart, and respected so much that I even get the same amount of it when they're not around. You would never be able to tell they were the BOSS unless someone told you. The two of them were very humble and weren't the flashy type of niggas. They supported all the kids in the community and didn't mind helping out those in need. But do either of them wrong and that was your life.

Akeem stood about six-two, weighing about two

hundred and twenty pounds. His body was cut into the perfect V. He had light hazel eyes with that dark caramel complexion that makes him look Hispanic or Dominican. His mom was mixed with black and white and his dad was full African. He had a Caesar haircut and his sideburns connected to the small goatee he was currently growing. He had a small dimple in the middle of his chin and his smile was perfect. Aiden resembled him a lot, minus the sideburns and goatee. These brothers were fine as hell and all the women went crazy over them.

Akeem and I met four years ago in high school. I was a new student and fresh meat. He was a senior on his way out, but once he and I met we clicked the moment we spoke to each other. Ever since then, we'd been riding for one another. I loved the benefits I received from being his girl as far as cars, shopping sprees, and endless money. Akeem was also my first at everything and taught me a lot.

"Hey baby. Is Brea asleep yet?"

"Go ahead with that baby shit, Farrah. You know we ain't rocking like that anymore."

"Why are you being mean to me?"

"Farrah, I've been telling you for the last few months this shit ain't working, yet you come climb your ass in my bed every night trying to fuck. Yea, I messed up a few times and gave it to you, but that by no means, means I want you back."

"Akeem, why is it that you don't want me? One day we're fine and the next day you're saying you don't want to be bothered. Is there someone else?"

"Here you go with your shit. Why when a man breaks up with a woman it automatically means he found someone else? I don't have time for no one right now. I'm stretching myself thin just to be with my daughter and you know she's everything to me."

"I remember when I was your everything, too."

"Yea, you were, until you fucked up and lost yourself in my money."

"What you mean I lost myself?"

"I mean you have no ambition or goals to get out there and do your own thing. You would rather spend and shop all day than find something to occupy your time."

"What's wrong with that?"

He shook his head laughing but I didn't see anything funny.

"Nothing, Farrah. Just make sure you check on my daughter before you hop on your phone to look online at those dumb social sites," he said and finished getting dressed.

Akeem wasn't into the social network. He claimed it didn't do anything but cause problems between family, friends, and spouses. I sat on the bed and watched him get ready to go out. There was no need to stay up because I probably wouldn't see him again until the sun came up.

Aiden

After Akeem dropped me off, I went straight in the bathroom to jump in the shower. I had this chick coming over that I met a few months ago. She and I'd been texting all day about now she wanted to come see me. Now what kind of man would I be if I didn't give a woman what she wanted? I dried myself off, threw some sweats and a wife beater on. Put some lotion and cologne on because women loved that shit, and took my ass downstairs to get something to drink. As I was going into the kitchen, my phone vibrated and it was the chick telling me she was outside. I opened the door and she stood there, smiling.

This chick wasn't a bad bitch, but she was cute. She stood about five-foot-six and was light-skinned with normal brown eyes. Her body wasn't all that and I could tell she had a small pouch around her stomach when I hugged her. Her thighs were what drew me to her. They were nice and thick just the way I liked them and her ass was just right, too. There was something about the way she smiled that made me want to get to know her.

"Are you going to let me in or do I have to stand here until you finish staring?"

Yea she had a smart-ass mouth too, but that was just for the time being. If I kept her around, that shit was going to stop.

"My bad. You look nice." I told her stepping over to the side so she could come in. I closed the door behind her and she

17

handed me a small gift bag. I glanced up at her because we'd only been kicking over the phone for a short period of time. This was her first time here and she was bringing me gifts.

"Just open it, silly."

She followed me in the other room and watched me. After I moved all that damn tissue paper, I found a bottle of Hennessy with a red bow on it and an envelope with twenty-five dollars in it to our local liquor store.

"Why would you give me money?" I handed it back to her but she refused to take it.

"I didn't know what type of liquor you drank and my sister told me not to come empty handed because it was rude."

I sat the bag down on the table and pulled her up close to me. I placed a soft kiss on her lips and then her neck. I heard the quiet moan that left her mouth and grinned. Woman loved that shit.

"Thanks, baby girl. I appreciate the thought."

"Are you going to give me a tour?"

I grabbed her hand and showed her my house. All six bedrooms, four baths, the backyard, garage, and anywhere else she wanted to see. When it was all said and done, we ended up in my room talking about everything and watching something on Netflix. Shorty was mad cool and I wanted to get to know her some more. She dozed off while lying there. I heard her phone ring and it was someone named Phoenix calling her. I don't know why, but I got mad another nigga was calling her. I woke her up and told her to answer her phone.

"Arizona, your phone is ringing." She stirred in her sleep a little. I nudged her again until she woke up.

"Hello."

She ran her hand over my hair while she sat on the phone. I couldn't hear the person on the other end, but she quickly stopped and jumped up.

"I'm on my way."

She put her shoes on and ran downstairs to grab her purse.

"Yo, you good?"

"Yea, I have to go handle something. I'll call you."

She pecked my lips with hers and ran out the room. I ain't going to lie, a nigga felt some kind of way. That's usually my excuse for leaving a woman's house. I don't know what's up with that, but I was definitely finding out who this Phoenix person was.

I walked shorty to her car and gave her a peck on the lips. I wasn't about to get all into a deep kiss and she was leaving. When she pulled off, I locked up and went upstairs to see my phone ringing back-to-back.

"Yo."

"Hey baby. You want some company?"

"Only if you trying to fuck."

"Damn, Aiden. It's like that."

"It sure is. You coming to fuck or not?"

She told me yes and hung up. Cassie was my ex who I broke up with some months ago because she was just like my brother's ex. You know the type of woman who thought because she had some good pussy and you had money, she didn't have to do anything with her life. I didn't have a problem with my woman sitting back spending my money, if she had my kids or was doing something with her life. But sitting on social media, posting pictures of your body is not a job.

Cassie was a beautiful woman. I'm talking video vixen, Instagram model type beautiful, but her attitude was fucked up. She thought every woman wanted me and would cut a fool in the clubs if she saw me conversing with one, just like she did with Arizona and Phoenix. After two years of that and her not wanting to do shit, I had enough and started doing me. I don't do that social media shit, but I do know people that do and they showed me all the stuff Cassie posted. That was another reason I left her ass. You aren't supposed to be showing other niggas what I got.

A half hour later, she was at my door wearing basically nothing. She stepped in and dropped her jacket to show me her new lingerie, I guess. The shit was all-black and see through.

"You coming?" she asked, walking up my steps. I watched her ass go from side-to-side and my dick grew.

"Hell yea."

She was taking the little she had on off when my phone

rang. I didn't even pay attention when I answered it. It was Shorty that just left and Cassie ass was being smart as usual by talking shit in the background. I could hear the hurt in Arizona's voice. I was going to make it up to her tomorrow, but right now I was about to get my dick wet.

Arizona

After my sister called I ran out of Aiden's house to find her. She told me my mom had to go back into rehab. You see, my mom was addicted to prescription drugs. She was in an accident a few years ago and lost her leg from the knee down and now she walked with a prosthetic. She was embarrassed and fell into a deep depression, causing her to become addicted to OxyContin, Vicodin, and any other medications she could get. It got so bad sometimes she would drink an entire bottle of Nyquil just to get some sort of feeling. I pulled up at our house and found the ambulance was there with two cops. My mom was in handcuffs screaming and shouting. The EMTs finally sedated her and got her to calm down. It was always a struggle getting her to the rehab place.

"Why are the cops here?" I asked my sister, who had tears running down her face. She was older than me by two years and the strong one, so to see her crying hurt my heart.

"I can't do this anymore. If mommy doesn't get it right this time, I'm moving out," she said, walking back in the house.

"You're just going to leave me?"

"Of course not bookie. You know I would never leave you."

After the cops and EMTs left with my mom, I sent the dude Aiden a text telling him I was sorry for running out of there and I would make it up to him. When he didn't text back, I figured he was mad. I called him up on the phone to see if he would answer.

"Hello," he sounded asleep.

"Hi Aiden. I'm sorry for running out I had and family emergency. Can I make it up to you?"

"It's all good."

"Hang the phone up, Aiden," I heard a female's voice say in the background. I looked at the phone to make sure I wasn't hearing shit.

"Damn. Aiden you didn't waste any time."

"It's not like that, baby girl."

"It's not like that, huh? I can't tell listening to the woman in the background. Handle your business and I will see you around."

I hung the phone up and fell back on my bed. I was mad as hell. I was really falling for him and thought he was the one. I met Aiden a few months ago coming out of the mall. He was tall, sexy, and so sweet. He and I would text on the phone all day, every day from the moment we met. It was like we knew each other mentally before physically and that was hard to find. We never talked about sex or anything in regards to it.

Today was the first day I was at his house because he was always busy and school took up a lot of my time. I admit when he invited me over, I was nervous. Yea, I had boyfriends before, but not any thug type ones like him. I told my sister all about him and she said bring him a gift. I didn't know people did that, but my sister said it was the gesture that people appreciated and she was right. When he pecked my lips and kissed my neck, I thought I would need the bathroom by the way he had me leaking. His kiss was soft and sensual and we didn't even let our tongues meet. Now here I was calling to make it up to him and he's laid up with some bitch, probably making her scream.

"Hey bookie. You ok?"

My sister had been calling me that since we were young. I told her what happened and she said it was best that I found out now what type of dude he was instead of finding out later when I was in too deep. But it was too late. I was already in too deep with Aiden. I wouldn't say I was in love with him, but I definitely felt something for him that's almost love. I guess texting and talking all day can make you fall for someone without being in their presence. She and I spoke a little more before I told her I was going to bed.

The next morning, I heard "U got it bad" by Usher playing on my phone and it was either a text or call from Aiden. That was the song I had set for him on my phone. I picked my phone up and it was a text message telling me he was sorry and to look outside. I threw the covers back, and instead of looking, I went out to see what it was. There were at least four dozen roses on my car with a card and a teddy bear. I picked all of it up and brought it back in my house. I wanted to be mad, but I didn't have the right when he wasn't my man. I smelled the roses and sent him a text.

24

Me: *Thank you Aiden but you didn't have to. And how do you know where I live?*

Aiden: *I'm glad you like it and don't worry about all that. Just be ready for me to take you out to breakfast in an hour.*

Me: *I guess.*

Aiden: *You guess. Don't make me come drag you out the bed.*

I decided to fuck with him.

Me: *What makes you think I want to get out of bed for you?*

Aiden: *You can stay in bed if you want. I'll bring breakfast to you baby girl. You tell me what's up.*

I couldn't help but smile. I told him to text me when he was outside. I didn't want to keep playing like that and he have me say something I couldn't get out of. I ran in my sister's room and jumped on her bed, telling her what happened.

"Ok. Be careful, sis. I know you're feeling him a lot, but don't let him off the hook easy. Make sure you let him have it without being ghetto about it. Let him know you demand respect and just because you ran home didn't mean he should've run to another woman."

"Do I have the right to say that? He's not my man."

"It doesn't matter. You like him right?" I nodded my head. "Then you have to let him know from the beginning you're not that type of chick that's going to allow a man to walk

25

all over you. The minute you do that, he'll always do it. I love you sis, now go get ready before you be saying I'm the one that made you late."

I kissed her cheek and ran to the bathroom. When I handled my hygiene, I put Vanilla lotion all over my body. I threw on some dark skinny jeans with a thin sweater than came off the shoulder and some ankle boots. I put my hair in a ponytail and put on a small amount of makeup. He sent the text to tell me he was outside. I stepped out and he was leaned up against the truck he was driving, talking on the phone. I don't even want to describe what he had on. Just know his ass was looking sexy as hell.

"Come here," he said and I moved into his embrace. His cologne smelled so good I didn't want to let go.

"I'm sorry. Do you forgive me?" He kissed my lips softly.

"Look Aiden. I'm just going to put it all out there before I get in your car and you can decide what you want to do."

He crossed his arms in front of him and waited for me to speak.

"Aiden, I'm sure you have a lot of women at your beck and call, but I'm not one of them. I'm not going to lie, I like you Aiden, probably more than I should. But I'm not trying to get my heart broken. I'm not into you sleeping with me and tossing me to the side until next time. I'm not asking you to be my man or anything like that, but if you don't see yourself

26

being with someone like me then you can just go. I would rather step away now than continue something that you don't see yourself doing and I get hurt in the end." He didn't respond to what I'd said. He just told me to get in the car. At first I wasn't but fuck it, he was treating and I was starving. If he didn't want to be with me like that, it was fine. At least I got a meal out of it.

Phoenix

Today was going to be a bad day, I could already tell. First I was running late, and second my car acted like it didn't want to start. I sent my sister a message telling her I had her car and would pick her up on my lunch break if she needed it. She told me not to worry about it because Aiden said he was kidnapping her today. I got a kick out of that because she was falling for him. I hope he did my sister right, because a bitch like me didn't have a problem fucking a nigga up. My sister was in her last year of college and I wasn't about to let him or anyone else make her lose focus, so he better be worth it.

I was sitting at the light when I felt someone staring at me. He was fine as hell, but once I looked at his car I knew he was a dope boy. He had to be driving a Maserati or Lamborghini with some spinning rims. I admit the car was nice as hell and the driver could get it, but I'd had enough of dealing with a dope boy. The last one I was with took me through the ringer. Bitches calling constantly, fighting him and them, and a bunch of other shit. He smiled and licked his lips. The shit was so sexy I didn't realize the light changed until I heard a horn. I made it my business to turn the corner even though I wasn't going that way. I could see him getting me into all sorts of trouble and those are problems I just didn't need.

I pulled up to work, which was at the check-cashing place. I was the manager there and had been for the last two years. There was a general manager over me, but she traveled a lot monitoring the spots. I went in through the back, turned everything on, and started counting out the cash to get ready for the day. Today went by slowly just like every day, but it was good money and paid the damn bills.

"Hey bookie," I sung in the phone when my sister called me.

"Phoenix, Aiden invited me to a surprise birthday party for his brother and I don't want to go alone. Can you go with me? Please."

"Sis, I had plans tonight."

"What plans? Sitting on the couch watching television and eating ice cream."

"Don't judge me," I said laughing in the phone.

"Come on, sis. Please, please."

I let her beg and gravel for a few minutes before I gave in. I was going to go the minute she asked. It had been a while since I'd been out.

"I'll meet you at the house when I get off."

"I should be there by then."

"What you mean you should be?"

"Well Aiden is taking me shopping for an outfit and getting me pampered, as he says, but I think he's making up for last night."

"Well, ok then. I think I have something new in my closet to wear. I'll see you later on."

We said our goodbyes and I went back to work. It was

29

finally eight and time for me to go home. I locked up the place and drove home listening to the old Mary J. Blige. I may be young, but her albums were the shit in the nineties.

I went in my house to get dressed and saw my Yorkie waiting at the door for me to take him out. After I fed and walked him, I went in my closet to find something to wear. I didn't know this dude, but if it was a surprise party I most likely needed to be dressed. I took out my nude bondage dress I'd just bought online from BeBe and my nude Coach heels. I hopped in the shower and hurried to get dressed because my sister was on her way. I put some mousse in my wet hair and let it curl up. I hated wearing makeup so I put on some lip-gloss and took a look at myself in the mirror.

I was what some men called slim thick. I was five-four with caramel skin and I had dark brown eyes. My chest was a C-cup, my waist was small, and my ass sat up lovely. Not Nicki Minaj lovely, but good enough. I had an earring on my lip and five small diamond ones going up and down my ears.

"Phoenix, you ready?" I heard my sister yell up the steps as I finished.

"I'm coming, bookie."

I walked downstairs and my sis was decked the hell out. She had on a black fitted dress with long sleeves and a split down her chest, showing off some cleavage. The shoes had to be red bottoms because they had that snake on the heel. I'd been wanting those forever! Her hair was parted down the

30

middle and her makeup was freshly done. She had on a necklace that could blind anyone, with earrings and bracelet to match. People often said my sister resembled the singer Tinashae, but sexier and thicker.

"Damn, sis. He did all that for you."

"He better had now that he's my man."

My mouth dropped open.

"Well how the hell did that happen?"

"After I went off on him a little this morning, he decided that I was worth the risk and asked me to be his girl over breakfast. I was scared at first, but hey what's the motto Drake says. YOLO."

"Oh shit."

I opened the door and she was driving a Mercedes Benz S550 or something like that.

"I know. He knew you had my car and told me to drive this. Do you think it's too much? I mean he just asked me to be his girl and he's spoiled me enough today to last me a lifetime."

"It's not too much if he has it. But just remember who you are. Don't let him start thinking you need him. Yes, these gifts are extravagant and all, but they can all be taken away just as quick. But tonight enjoy it, bookie."

She nodded her head and we headed over to the club. It was beyond packed when we got there. Of course we missed the birthday guy walk in, but who cares. She and I found a table close to the dance floor so we could dance, leave our things at the table, and still see them.

"Hey, baby," I heard a voice behind us. I turned around and the guy I'm assuming to be Aiden kissed my sister. This nigga was fine as hell. He was decked out in a suit and some gator shoes. I could smell his cologne from where I sat.

"Hey to you. I want you to meet my sister, Phoenix." He smiled and shook my hand.

"Oh, you're Phoenix?" he smiled while shaking my hand.

"The one and only."

"Phoenix. And you're Arizona. What was your mom thinking?"

We all laughed because we got that all the time. My mom always told us that's where she wanted to go one day when she was younger. She never had the money, so when she had us we got the joy of being named after the city and state she loved.

"Damn baby, you're the best looking woman in here. Well you and your sister are," he said and started kissing her neck. I watched him gawk over my sister and her enjoy every moment.

"Ugh, excuse me Aiden."

We heard a voice say behind him. He turned around and a scowl was on his face instantly.

"What the fuck you want?" he said to the chick that seemed aggravated by his answer.

"How you over here with this bitch and you were just with me last night?"

See, this is the foolery I wasn't beat for.

"Go 'head with that shit, yo. She already knows about that so you coming over here trying to blow my spot up ain't going to work. Get the fuck on before you have a problem on your hands."

"Fuck you and those bitches."

That was all it took and I was on her ass beating the shit out of her. The one thing my sister and I don't tolerate is chicks calling us bitches, especially when we didn't do shit. I get she was mad, but take that shit up with him.

"Get off me Aiden, that's my sister," I heard Arizona yelling in the back of me. Usually we would fuck chicks up together so I knew she was mad she didn't get any hits in. I felt a pair of strong arms lift me up in the air.

"Get that bitch out of here," I heard the person say that lifted me up. He stood me up and I pulled my dress down. I glanced around the club and felt embarrassed, but didn't care.

"I'm not going to ask if you're ok because you beat the shit out of her. But do you need anything?"

"Nah, I'm good," I answered before looking up. When I did I was staring into the eyes of the same guy I saw driving earlier. His smile was hypnotizing and his body was ridiculously ripped from what I felt.

"Let me get you a drink."

"No thanks. I'm about to leave." I looked for my sister and Aiden had her sitting in his lap smiling from ear-to-ear.

"Already. Damn the birthday boy can't get a dance?"

"Happy Birthday. One dance and I'm out."

He took my hand and we ended up dancing for more than one song. The way his body moved with mine had me feeling like taking him home and having a one-night stand. My inner hoe was definitely trying to break free.

"Really, Akeem? You don't invite me to your party and then I get here and you hugged up with some bitch."

Why were these hoes testing me tonight? He must've known I was getting mad because he moved me behind him.

"Fuck out of here, Farrah. We aren't together and I don't have to tell you shit."

"We're not together. Who's lying in bed with you every night? Who's sucking and fucking you all day, every day?"

She started talking more crap and I walked off. I know she was saying that for me to hear, but I was good on that. He may have been sexy, but drama was not about to follow me and that's exactly what she was. I went and sat back down with my sister to tell her I was leaving.

"Aiden, nothing better not happen to her while I'm gone."

"Ain't nothing going to happen that she doesn't want to," he said and I knew what his nasty ass was talking about. I hoped my sister was ready because once she went down that road with him, there was no turning back.

Steel

I was dancing with some chick that just finished beating up Aiden's ex when Farrah tried to show her ass. I saw shorty balling her fist up and moved her behind me. When she stepped off, I yanked Farrah up and had Finn, who is one of my loyal soldiers, take her home. Today was my birthday and she was fucking it up. I looked around the club for the woman and saw her with my brother and his new girlfriend. I met her today and she seemed pretty cool and laid back. Not anything I'm used to seeing Aiden with. When he called me and said he wanted me to meet her, I was skeptical. No one knew this woman and he was making her his girl.

"Can I talk to you for a minute?" I asked the chick.

"I'm not interested." She waved me off and stood up to leave. Now that I got a good look at her, she was pretty but she wasn't the baddest chick I'd ever seen.

"Not interested in what? I just asked to talk to you."

"Like I said, I'm not interested."

"Damn, it's like that?"

"Yea it's like that. I don't have time or energy to waste on a man who has a woman stalking him like that," I laughed because it did look like that's what Farrah did.

"Look, I'm not these other niggas you can talk to like that."

"And why is that?"

"Because I'm the man your mom warned you about. I'm

36

that nigga to upgrade you and make other women envy and want to be you. I have the means of making you a BOSS bitch."

"No thanks. I'm ok with my corny life. I don't need to be upgraded or envied. I'm fine just the way I am. If you'll excuse me."

She tried to move past me and I stopped her.

"Oh what, you too good to be a BOSS bitch?"

"That's the second time you used the word bitch referring to me. I know right now that I'm not the woman for you because my man, or my Boss man, ain't about to call me out my name."

"You know how many women would love to be on my arm or have me upgrade them? You may be pretty but you're not the baddest chick in here."

"Good, then you don't need me. Be my guest and have your pick of the litter. I'm sure they're all just waiting for you to choose them, bro."

"Hold up. Did she just bro me?"

"She sure did," Aiden said laughing.

"Oh, hell no."

"What you going to do, yoke me up like you did your little stalker? Bye, sis."

She waved at her sister. I grabbed her arm and pressed her up against the wall. She tried to push me off and failed. I'd never met a woman in my twenty-five years give me attitude like her. I usually had them throwing themselves all over me, but not her.

"You can play tough all you want, but I know for a fact this is what you want and I'm going to give it to you when the time is right. Until then, you're going to control that little attitude you have."

I put my hand behind her neck and moved in closer. I kissed her lips then sucked on them and tasted that cherry lip gloss she wore. Her arms went around my neck and I could tell she wanted to wrap her legs around my waist by the way she lifted them up. I placed my finger under her chin and gave her another kiss on her neck and that's when I heard it. Yup, that soft moan that let me know she wanted me just as bad as I wanted her.

"I'm about to go slide up in some pussy, but I want you to meet me for lunch tomorrow."

I could see the look of disgust in her face. Fuck it, though. I was always honest when I met a chick.

"You tried it. You better hope that pussy is worth it because that's who you'll be having lunch with tomorrow."

She tried to walk off again and I snatched her back.

"I better see you or we are going to have problems," I whispered in her ear. I let my hand roam up and down her legs. I stopped when I reached her prized possession and felt how wet she was through her panties.

"You playing tough but you like this shit. Don't you?"

She didn't answer so I sped my pace up and circled her pearl faster. I could tell she was enjoying it by the way she hid her face in my chest and the speed of her breathing.

"I don't hear you," I couldn't even say her name because I didn't know it.

"Yes. Yes," she moaned in my ear. And just as she was about to let go, I stopped. Her eyes popped open.

"Why did you stop?" she put my hand back down there to finish and I snatched it back.

"You don't deserve this yet. I'm going to make you beg for it."

She lifted her hand and smacked me. Now usually if anyone did that you would never see them again, but something about the way she did it turned me on. I saw her grab her stuff up and storm out.

"What did you do to my sister? She doesn't go around smacking people," her sister stood in front of me with her arms folded. I stood there looking at her, and she was just as pretty as her sister.

"What's up, Boss? You need me to handle that one for you?" My other soldier Rowan said. I saw Aiden's girl mouth drop open.

"You better not send them to hurt my sister."

I saw her storm off behind her.

"Damn Akeem. I know damn well she ain't coming home with me now. You just had to throw that Boss shit out

39

there with Phoenix." So that was her name.

"What? She act like she was too good."

"You funny as hell, nigga. Let me go find a chick to wet my dick up too, then," he said.

"Hold up I thought that was your girl."

He gave me a look that said "and". I ended up going to a hotel with two chicks, but my mind stayed on the Phoenix chick all night. Yes, I know who I was fucking, but my thoughts were clouded with who I wanted to be fucking. I woke up with too many messages from Farrah and two women on each side of me. I looked at the time and it was a little after nine. I had those chicks get up and get ghost.

Arizona

I ran behind my sister for two reasons: to make sure she was ok and because I was her ride. I thought for sure Aiden would come check on me to make sure I was good, but I guess not. I planned on going to his house tonight and let him be my first. Yes, I was a virgin and proud of it. I thought about giving it away to my last boyfriend, but I changed my mind when he sat me down and told me he was gay. I'm not ashamed to admit that, either. He was the one in the closet, not me. I knew it wasn't anything wrong with my vagina to make him to turn men because he never had it. I figured that was something he was into. I didn't judge him and to this day we're like best friends. Listen, it's too much going on in this world for me to worry about whose sleeping with whom. I parked in front of our house and turned the car off. Phoenix just sat there, staring out the window.

"What's up, sis? Why did you smack Aiden's brother like that?"

She had a sneaky ass grin on her face. When she told me what happened, I laughed so hard.

"Phoenix I can't believe you let him feel you up in the club like that."

"I know, right. But he was so cocky and arrogant that it turned me on instead of off."

We stayed out there talking for an hour when I told her I was on my way to Aiden's. I sent him a text to tell him I

41

would be waiting for him at the house.

"You sure you want to go without him texting you back first. That's the number one rule when messing with a dude like him."

"What is?"

"Don't do pop-up visits. If he doesn't call or text you back, it means he's busy and you should probably wait."

"I would go with that rule if he didn't give me the key. You really think he would have a chick over there when he just gave me this?"

"I guess. But if you need me, call and I'll be right there. Where did you say he lived again?"

I gave her his address and hugged her. Once she got in the house, I pulled off to take my twenty-minute drive to see my man.

I pulled in his driveway and didn't see his car. I was happy because it gave me time to get myself ready for him. I opened the door and went to his mini-bar to pour myself a drink. I took my heels off and sat on the couch. I was a nervous wreck. I took a few shots and made my way up the stairs.

"Fuck Aiden, that's the third one. I can't take any more."

I froze when I heard a woman saying that. Now, I had two choices. One was to barge in there and flip the fuck out and two was just leave because that's something I didn't want to see.

"Yes baby. I'm cumming again," I heard her say and felt the tears falling.

I backed up from the door and chose the latter. Yea I heard her moaning and saying his name, but it's nothing like seeing it. I ran downstairs without making any noise and called Phoenix and told her to come get me. I left his car and key. If this is what I would be dealing with being with a man like him, I'll pass. I didn't want him to come out and see me, so I started walking down the street. Fifteen minutes later, my sister jumped out the car and hugged me.

"Why would he do that, Phoenix? Who ask someone to be his girl and cheats on her all on the same day? I should've known better."

"It's ok, sis. I know you were really feeling him, but its better you found out now. Did you whoop both of their asses?"

"I couldn't find it in me to open the door. Just hearing her moan out Aiden's name had my stomach turning. That was supposed to be me, Phoenix, experiencing my first time. I know we only known each other a few months, but that was my man."

"What you want to do? I can turn around and we can go fuck shit up. Just give me the ok and it's done."

I loved my sister because we had each other's back, no matter what.

"No, I don't want to see him anymore. Is that being childish?"

"Ugh no. Who wants to see a cheating ass nigga?"

"Too bad I didn't see who the chick was. I bet it was the one you beat up at the club."

"Fuck this," I heard her say and she turned the car around.

"What are we doing here?"

We were parked at the next-door house to Aiden's.

"We're going to sit out here and see who the bitch is. Don't worry he won't see us."

I nodded my head and sent him a message.

Me: *I guess I wasn't what you needed after all. I came by to surprise you and got more than I bargained for. Thank goodness I didn't sleep with you or it probably would've hurt more. Anyway, I hope you got your nut. Lose my number asshole."*

I showed it to Phoenix and hit send. We were both cracking up when we noticed his door opened. It looked like they were arguing about something when a cab pulled up.

"Damn, she can't even get a ride home. What a fuck nigga," Phoenix said.

We couldn't see that well and took our phones out. We zoomed in on her phone and wouldn't you know it, it was the same chick from the club. We may not have seen her face perfectly, but she had the same outfit on and her hair was the same. She got in the cab and that must be when he noticed his car I'd left in the driveway. He looked around the car and ran

44

back in the house where I'm assuming he found his key.

"Give it a minute, sis."

"What you mean?" I had no idea what she was talking about.

"Five, four, three, two, and one," she pointed to my phone that started ringing and pulled off. I looked down and it was Aiden.

"How did you know he was going to call?"

"Easy. He just noticed the car was there and the key. I can bet he checked his phone and saw the message and dialed you. Now the question is, what are you going to do when he comes over?"

"Huh? How do you know he's coming over?"

"Trust me, he is."

"Drop me off at Brian's house. You have his key on you? If not, take mine."

She gave me hers because mine was home on my key ring. We both had a key to his house and he had one to ours. She dropped me off at Brian's, which was only around the corner from us.

I went in his guest bedroom, showered, and laid down. I looked at my phone and had thirty-six missed calls and a few texts apologizing and asking me to call him. I was good on that.

"Hey bookie, I'm just calling to tell you that nigga just left."

"Oh my goodness, he came."

"Yup."

She was about to tell me what happened but Brian came in and sat down on the bed. I told her I would call her in the morning. He asked me what happened and when I told him, he smacked me on the back of the head.

"What?"

"Are you crazy messing with a nigga like Aiden?"

I didn't see what the big deal was about him and his brother. But I guess everyone else did.

"Him and his brother are those type of niggas that should only mess with ratchet bitches. Those are the ones who can deal with them, but even then, it's hard. Boo, you are a good girl and I don't want to see you hurt, but you need to let that one go."

I finished telling him what happened and he pulled me in for a hug.

"Is that him?" I nodded my head yes. My phone was ringing off the hook from Aiden.

"He doesn't know where you are, does he?"

"No. And no, I don't have find my iPhone on."

"Shut it off."

"Why?"

"Girl, you are clueless. He is the type of nigga that don't need an app to find you. That man is a Boss and the sooner you realize that, the better. Now go to bed. We'll talk some more in the morning." I heard everything he said. *But what is he a boss of?*

I thought about how I was ready to give him all of me. Thank goodness I didn't.

Aiden

After Arizona ran after her sister, I went to look for another chick to take home. I know a nigga ain't shit, but I also know Arizona wasn't ready to sleep with someone like me. She was a good girl and I was going to wait for her to be ready. Unfortunately, the liquor took over and I needed to slide up in something.

I looked down at my phone that was ringing and it was Cassie. *Bingo.*

I could fuck her and not have to stop at the store and pick up condoms because she was on the pill. Plus, I'm the only man she's been with for the last two years. And yes, I'm positive about that because I have eyes everywhere. Plus, she was too scared of losing me, which she did anyway.

When I met Arizona at the mall, I didn't want to jump into anything being I had just got out of a relationship. Arizona and I would kick it on the phone until the wee hours of the morning, and then text all day. I started falling for her and I knew it, but refused to admit it out loud. The day she came over and we talked, I realized she was just what I needed in my life.

The day I picked her up for breakfast, I took her to meet my brother to see what he thought of her. The two of them seemed to hit it off, but the one I needed to her to get along with was my mom. Akeem and I always said if our mom doesn't like them, we can't fuck with them like that.

Unfortunately, my mom found out too late about Farrah and Cassie. Anyway, I'd mentioned her to my mom and she told me to bring her by which I planned on doing tomorrow.

After I finished fucking Cassie, she started asking if we were going to get back together and who was the bitch I was with at the club. I called her ass a cab quick and sent her on her way. I was going to shower and stop by to see my girl, but it looked like she got to me first. I checked my car to see if she keyed it. I was hoping she dropped it off and left. I ran in the house and saw the key. Still not thinking she did until I saw the message. I felt like shit because she heard or saw me sleeping with my ex, either way that shit had to hurt. I made her my girl this morning and cheated on her tonight.

I called her phone back-to-back and when she didn't answer, I flew over there. Her sister opened the door with her face turned up and told me to stop banging on her door. I got a kick out of her. I couldn't wait for my brother to tame her ass. She told me Arizona wasn't there, so I passed right by her and checked the entire house. I left and picked my phone up to call my boy and had him trace her phone. I don't care about that find my iPhone app. My boy could find your phone at the last place you turned it off at and that's why I'm sitting around the corner from her house in front of some guy named Brian's place. Here she found me with another chick, and she was at some dude's house. I had to get myself together before I went to the door.

"She's in the other room."

He didn't even ask who I was, which told me she told him about me. He pointed to the room she was in and I opened the door and stood there. I could hear her sniffling.

"Brian, I thought you said we would talk in the morning."

"It isn't Brian."

I could tell I scared her by the way she jumped out the bed. She had on some small shorts and a tank top. Her breasts were just about popping out and her hair was all over her head.

"What are you doing here, Aiden?"

"What do you mean why am I here? I'm here for you."

"Well you can go back to her because I'm done with you."

I moved in closer to her and she put her arm out to stop me.

"Just tell me why?"

"Why what Arizona?"

"Why did you ask me to be your girl and have sex with someone else the same night? Is it because she's prettier than me or has a better body? Why would you do that to me?"

"Hell no, that's not the reason. Arizona, I like you just the way you are. You left and I was drunk and horny. I was being stupid and I'm sorry."

"Do you know how it feels to hear a woman moaning out the name of the guy you're falling in love with? No, I'm

50

sure you don't. Maybe I should let you walk in on some shit like that."

"Arizona don't ever let those words leave your mouth again. I'm not that type of nigga you want to threaten."

"Huh? I didn't threaten you."

And that's when I knew she was the one. She had no idea who I was or how bad I was for her. She only saw me and nothing else.

"You're falling in love with me, Ari?"

"Who the hell is Ari? Are you really calling me someone else's name?"

"No baby. That's what I'm going to call you for now on. That's your nickname."

"Whatever."

"Don't whatever me and answer the question."

"What question? Back up Aiden, you are too close."

I moved in closer and asked her again.

"Are you falling in love with me, Ari?"

I had her nervous as hell. I kissed her forehead, then her lips and her neck.

"Mmmmm," she moaned out and I smiled.

"Answer me."

"No. I'm not telling you anything," she said and scooted underneath my arm. It didn't matter, she'd said it. I just wanted to hear it again. She opened the door in the bedroom to escort me out.

"Get your shit. You're coming home with me."

"No I'm not. You think you can come over here and get me hot and bothered and all is forgiven. Hell no. Take your ass home by yourself and I'll think about calling you."

"I'm going to allow you to talk to me like that this one time because I hurt you and I deserve it, but don't let it happen again. I expect to hear from you today."

"Whatever."

"Arizona, don't test me. You don't want to see that side."

"Well maybe you don't want to see my bad side, either," she said trying not to laugh. I looked at her and we both started cracking up. I picked her up and kissed her lips.

"Put me down, fool."

"Can I stay the night with you since you won't come with me?"

I could tell she was fighting it, so I grabbed her hand and led her back to the bed. I took my shoes off and got in behind her. The shit felt so right being with her. This was definitely going to be the last time I fucked up with her.

"Aiden."

"Yea babe."

"If, and I mean if, I decide to take you back I'm not coming to your house until everything that bitch touched, laid on, and bathed with is out in the trash."

I couldn't do shit but laugh but I was going to make sure to have that handled first thing.

"You got that."

"I better."

"I hear you," I said trying to go to sleep.

"And…"

"Go to sleep, Ari."

"Don't cut me off."

"I'm not. We can talk in the morning."

She snuggled up under me and was sleep in less than five minutes and I wasn't too far behind her. The next day, I woke up and she was still asleep. I looked at my phone and it was after nine. I had missed calls from my brother and some from Cassie. I kissed Ari on the forehead and watched her stir a little in her sleep. I stepped out the bedroom and the dude was sitting at the island reading the paper.

"Thanks, man. This is for your troubles," I handed him two stacks because that's all I had in my pocket.

"I don't want your money. I just want you to be good to her. She may be a little hood but she's not the type of hood girl that can deal with someone like you."

"That's exactly why I want to be with her. I don't need her to be hood or ratchet. I like her just the way she is."

I nodded my head and walked to my car. I picked up my phone and had my assistant order all new furniture for a few rooms and told her to send a few dozen roses and some edible arrangements to Arizona. I know she was about to make me work for her, so I may as well get started now.

Phoenix

It's been two weeks since my sister busted Aiden at the house. Between the two of them, they were getting on my damn nerves. If he wasn't over here, he was calling her phone and then mine if she wouldn't answer. I got a kick out of how he was sweating her. A nigga like him could have whomever he wanted, but my sister was the only one in his view right now. She was giving him her ass to kiss and that's what he gets. She told me she planned on taking him back, but he had to work for her and that's what he's been doing. She had roses daily, fruit, candy, cards, teddy bears and any other thing he wanted to get her. The kicker was the brand new Infiniti truck he got her. She refused to drive it though, and I understood why.

Today I was going to be working alone because the four staff I had, were sent to a training by the owner, whoever he was. The entire time I've worked here I've never seen the owner, and now he wanted to send my staff away. I ran the day just like normal and couldn't wait for the time to pass. It was eight-thirty and I started closing up two of the drawers so it wouldn't be much at nine when it was closing time. Two dudes walked in looking like they were up to no good. I could tell because neither one had anything in their hands nor they were looking around.

"Can I help you?" I was being nice and professional.

"Fuck you, bitch. Run me that money."

I smirked and folded my arms. I wish the fuck I would give him all the cash we had in here.

"Oh, she think the shit funny."

He let off a shot barely missing my head. I didn't let him know it scared me and bent down to get the money. I opened the door on the side and the minute one of them opened it, I hit his ass in the chest with a hot one. The other one was so shocked he tried to run, and I got his ass in leg. I wasn't trying to kill them, but they weren't robbing me either. I shut the door back, called the police and my manager, and finished counting the money. Once all this was over, I was taking my ass home to take a nice, hot bath. The manager called me back and said the owner was on the way. I was giving the officers a statement when in walked Aiden, my sister, and his brother.

"Oh my God sis, are you ok?"

"Yea, I'm good. I just want to go soak. Why are they here?"

"Girl, they own this place."

My eyes shot open when she said that. I could see Aiden's brother got a kick out of me not knowing that shit. The next thing I knew, the two dudes that robbed the store got up off the floor and the officers shook hands with Aiden and Steel.

"What the fuck?"

The one I shot in the chest took off his bulletproof vest and the other one was still going to need medical treatment. I looked over at Steel with anger in my eyes.

"Oh shit, bro. She's about to let your ass have it," Aiden said laughing and pulling my sister with him.

"Tell me you didn't set that shit up."

He stood in front of me with his arms folded.

"I had to. I needed to see if my manager was down to ride for her Boss and I have to say you passed with flying colors," he grinned, thinking the shit was cute.

"Are you fucking kidding me? What if I would've shot them in the face? That was real reckless of you."

I moved around him and he grabbed hold of my arm.

"If you shot him in the face, then he would be dead. As far as being reckless, that's the type of nigga I am. You ain't know. You better ask somebody."

I snatched away from him and picked my things up to leave. I stepped outside and there was a brand new champagne colored BMW truck with a bow on it. I turned around and my sister was smiling as she sat in the car with Aiden.

"I don't want it."

I got in my car and pulled off. Who did that nigga think he was buying me shit? He doesn't know me like that. Fuck I look like, some trick? I was over his cocky ass. He could kiss my ass. I parked in front of my house and got out. I let my dog out and started my bath water. Once my dog was in, I lit some candles, put Pandora on my phone to Mary J Blige radio, and zoned out. I felt the water getting cold so I turned the shower on to wash up and got out. This motherfucker was standing in my room leaning against the wall.

"I see leave me the fuck alone doesn't register in your brain. Do I need to say fuck off? Which one will get you to say fuck me?"

He moved closer to me, yanked my towel from around me, and left me standing there naked. I wasn't ashamed of my body, so I didn't mind. He licked his lips and just like that my back was against the wall with his tongue dancing with mine.

"Get off," I tried to push him away but the nigga had me about to cum off his fingers. "Is this what you want, Steel?"

He didn't say anything. I put my hands in his pants and snatched it back out when I felt that giraffe's neck he had down there. He looked up and smiled. I was able to make him lose focus and get from under him.

"If this is what you want Steel, come get it."

I sat on the bed with my legs spread open and started massaging my clit and my chest. He kneeled down in front of me and pulled me to the edge of the bed. I could feel his tongue go up and down my slit but he wasn't sucking on the most sensitive spot like I wanted him to. I tried to guide him there with my hips, but he stopped and stared at me.

"When you're ready to fuck with a Boss, call me. Until then handle that yourself," he said and walked the fuck out.

I threw my remote at him and I swore I heard him laugh. When my door slammed, I laid right there playing with myself. I had thoughts of the way he would fuck me and lose control and let loose. I came so hard I put myself to sleep. Fuck that nigga. If he wanted to play games, he could play them by himself.

Steel

I had Phoenix's ass right where I wanted her. She thought that attitude she had would make me leave her alone, but the shit didn't do anything but make me want her more. The truck was her sister's idea, but when she left it at the job that let me know my money couldn't help me with her. Aiden said her sister was the same way. Where the hell have they been hiding all this time? All I meet are women who want me for what I can do for them and that's fine because I'm supposed to be the provider, but damn can a nigga get a chick to pay for his food sometimes?

Today I promised my daughter I would take her out to eat, but she said her mom had to go. I know that was Farrah's ass making her do that. My daughter loved her daddy-daughter time, so when she asked for her mom to go, I knew it was a setup. I moved into my own house about a half hour from Farrah. The further, the better, if you asked me. I blew the horn when I got in their driveway.

My daughter came out wearing some jeans with those little riding boots and her shirt said "sexy". I was about to smack the hell out of Farrah. Who puts a damn shirt on a three-year-old like that? I'd made reservations at Brea's favorite spot, otherwise her ass would change that. I buckled her in the car seat and waited on her mom. Farrah came out in some sexy attire that got my dick hard, which I'm sure was on purpose. I looked at her and pulled out the driveway. We were enjoying our meal when I heard a voice that was too familiar.

"No, I don't have a man. If I did this wouldn't be happening," she told the guy as she pointed between the two of them.

"I miss you baby."

My head turned around so fast to see who she was talking to. It was this dude named Jett that worked for me down in South Jersey. He wasn't a Boss like me, but I gave him free reign to control shit down there.

"Where are you going, daddy?" My daughter Brea asked when I stood up.

"I'll be right back, baby. Eat those vegetables."

"Ok. Hurry back so I can finish telling you my story."

I kissed her cheek and made my way on the other side of the booth. I stood in front of her and she rolled her eyes.

"What up, Steel? It's been a while."

"Yea, it has. What's up Phoenix? Are you not going to speak?"

"For what?" she answered with an attitude. I chuckled and snatched her ass out the booth. Jett went to get up, but my facial expression made him sit back down. I pushed her towards the bathroom.

"You think this is a fucking game?"

"Is what a game, Steel? You're bugging."

"Nah, you ain't seen bugging yet."

"How the fuck you got me in the corner and your ass here with your stalker?" she pointed in her direction and Farrah was staring at me.

"My daughter is with us." I could tell she didn't believe me because she stood on her tippy toes to see.

"Hmph. That still doesn't give you a right to interrupt my date."

"Oh, that's a date?"

"Yes, it is. Now move, I'm being rude."

"Check this Phoenix," I turned her face to mine so she could see how serious I was. "You're going to go over there and tell Jett you have to go. I want you at my house by the time I get there."

She rolled her eyes.

"Phoenix."

"What?"

"Don't make me come looking for you, ma. I don't think you're ready for that."

She pushed past me with an attitude and went back to her seat. I gave Jett a head nod and went back to my seat. I heard her tell him she had to go and she would see him later. Little did she know, that was never happening. I know she didn't know where I lived so I had Rowan, who was outside, approach her and tell her to follow him. He and a few other people were the only ones who knew where my house was. I sent my brother a text and asked him if he could go open the door for her. Once he texted me "ok," I enjoyed the rest of my dinner with my daughter. I felt my ex burning a hole in me, but who cares.

"Daddy, can we do this again tomorrow?"

"Not tomorrow, but maybe the next day. Go inside with the nanny so I can talk to mommy for a second."

"Ok. I love you."

"I love you, too. Don't forget to call me before you go to bed," I kissed her cheek and watched the nanny take her inside.

"What's the problem now, Farrah?"

I opened up my message and smiled when Rowan told me she was in the house and he was waiting for me to get there.

"That right there is what's wrong with me."

I put my phone away and turned to her.

"What part don't you get, Farrah? We're not together. You want to have these family dates thinking it's going to make everything better and it's not. I don't want to be with you anymore. I left you the house, your three cars, you have help with the nanny and you still have an endless bank account for yourself because I have a separate account for you to spend on Brea. What else do you want?"

"I want you with all that. Please stay so we can work it out."

"Did you hear what you said? You still want me but with everything else. What would you do if you didn't have all that? Would you still want a nigga then?"

When she didn't answer, I kicked her ass straight out my ride. I don't even know why I wasted four years on a selfish bitch like her.

"Fuck you Steel, and that bitch you're about to run to."

"You got one thing right. I'm about to fuck the shit out of her. I'll let you know how it was."

She started kicking my ride and I pulled off, laughing. That's what her dumb ass gets. I opened the gate to my house and parked in my circular driveway. I walked up to Rowan's car and told him he could bounce. I went straight to my room to shower before I dealt with this crazy woman. She was in my bed watching television.

"Look who made themselves comfortable."

I went in the bathroom to get cleaned up. When I came out she was staring too hard if you ask me.

"What the fuck you staring at?"

She sucked her teeth, "Is that how you get women? I mean you're just so sweet."

She was being sarcastic, but I had something for her ass.

"I got you, didn't I?"

"Ugh, no. I was forced here."

"If you feel like you were forced, then bounce."

64

Farrah had pissed me off and she was doing the same.

"I could if I had a car motherfucker. You think I wanted to be stuck here waiting for a no good nigga who thinks he running shit."

"That's because I am, now strip," I was so close our faces almost touched. "What are you waiting for?"

"I'm not stripping. You got me fucked up."

I chuckled.

"I got you fucked up huh?"

I unbuckled her pants and she tried to stop me, but it didn't work. I removed her shirt and the rest of her clothes. The first time I saw her naked I was high and not really paying attention, but now that I saw her I was like DAMN. This chick was definitely bad.

"Now, what were you saying?"

"I didn't strip for you, did I?"

"I'm over you being tough. Let's see how tough you are when I throw all this dick on you."

I pushed her back on the bed and she tried to scoot away from me.

"Don't run, Phoenix. I'm about to make you eat those words."

I threw my tongue in her mouth before she could respond. I sucked on her entire body and found my way back down to her safe haven. My tongue went up and down her slit and she arched her back instantly. I blew, bit, and ate her pussy and ass until she couldn't cum anymore.

"Ok, Steel. I'm not going to say anything else. I can't cum anymore," she screamed out.

I got up after she released that last one that had her body flipping on the bed. I moved up and placed the head on her clit and she grinded her hips under me.

"Fuck Steel, put it in. I need to feel you," she moaned out and that shit turned me on. Women usually told me to go in slow. I eased in, and then pulled back out and she put her hand around my neck and wrapped her legs around my back.

"Stop playing, baby. Please."

"How bad do you want it?" I asked kissing her.

"As bad as you said I did."

I pushed my dick all the way in and the pleasure and pain I saw on her face was enough to drive me crazy. Her walls sucked in my dick and squeezed the hell out of it. I flipped her over just so I wouldn't cum. Her pussy was extremely gushy and making farting sounds. She threw her ass back and made it clap. This has to be the best sex I've ever encountered. A chick that can take all my dick and fuck me right. Yea, she was a keeper.

"Let me get on top baby."

I rolled over on my back and watched her go up and down, back and forth. I rubbed her clit until it got hard.

"Fuck yea, Phoenix. Ride that dick harder."

She started fucking the shit out of me on top. I couldn't let her out-sex me. I grabbed her hips and thrusted up in her as I made her go harder.

"Steel, I'm about to cum."

"Me, too. Cum with me."

"Oh shittttt."

"Fuckkkkk, Phoenix. That was best pussy I ever had and I'm not just saying that," I told her when she rolled off me.

"I can tell you that was definitely the best dick I ever had. I haven't had many but the few I did, that was by far the best."

"That's good to know."

"Yea."

She came out the bathroom and wiped my dick down and seconds later had her mouth wrapped around it, bringing him back to life. She didn't get all of it in right away but when she did, I felt like a bitch grabbing the sheets and moaning out her name. When I came, she made sure not to leave a drop.

"Come here," I pulled her up and kissed her aggressively until my dick was hard again.
I stood up and guided her down and fucked her against the wall, on the floor, dresser, an anywhere else I could in my bedroom. She and I fucked all night long. I was so drained afterwards we fell asleep naked. I woke up the next day and she was nowhere to be found. I picked my phone up to call her and her phone number was changed. *What the fuck just*

happened?

Farrah

I was so pissed when Steel told me he was about to go make love to that bitch. I went in the house and got my daughter ready for bed. I waited until she was asleep and called Steel all night long. I assume he left his phone somewhere besides his room because there was no way I was ringing him off the hook and he didn't at least turn it off. Thank goodness the nanny was there. I hopped in my car and pulled the iPhone app up and tracked his phone. I parked in front of this big ass mansion. This nigga was living it up while we stayed in the old house. Fuck that, I want this one. Yes, I was a gold digging bitch, but why shouldn't I be? He got it. I noticed he had a gate that needed a code to get in. Fortunately for me, it was open.

I got to the door and looked inside one of the side windows on the door. This house belonged in a fucking magazine. I noticed someone walking by and took my chances and knocked on the door. I was shocked to see a woman who seemed to be a maid. I was wondering what she was doing there, but I looked at my watch and it was six in the morning. She must've been coming to work.

I told her I was the lady of the house and her dumb ass believed me. I went straight upstairs to act like I belonged. I went from room to room. I got to a set of double doors and opened them. The room had to be half the size of a ballroom. It was huge. The bed sat up on a high platform and you needed to go up to the steps to get on it. The television was so big it resembled a movie screen. I scanned the entire room while they both laid there asleep.

I felt a pair of eyes on me and when I looked, it was her shaking her head. She stood up and the bitch was naked. I'm not gay, but her body was bad as hell. I could see cum dried up on the inside of her leg and got mad all over again. She came to where I was standing and stood in my face.

"Why are you here?" she whispered out. I decided to fuck with her.

"What you think you're the only one that fucked him in that bed? Bitch, you're not special. He's just having fun with you right now."

"Then why does he go out of his way to find me if this ain't what he want?"

"Duh, he just wanted to sample the pussy. Don't expect him to contact you after this. He told my daughter he was coming back home." He turned over in the bed and we both stopped talking.

"If he doesn't want you, why are you doing all this?"

"Listen boo. I see you are falling for him but the fact remains that I have his daughter and we're always going to be a family. Let me ask you this, have you met his mom yet?"

She shook her head no. "It's too soon to meet his mom."

"I met her the first day he met me."

I had her stupid ass thinking.

70

"You know what? This right here," she pointed to us back and forth. "This love triangle thing stops here. I'm good. If you want him, you can have him. I'm not about to deal with your stalking ass just to be with him."

She got her clothes and started putting them on. I saw her send a text to someone.

"I'm offended. Stalker. I call it a woman trying to keep her family together."

"Call it what you want, but it's stalking. I'm out," she grabbed the rest of her things and walked out the room. All the whispering we were doing, you think he would've woke up but his ass was a heavy sleeper. The only thing waking him up was someone giving him head or yelling in his face.

I closed the door behind me and went downstairs and saw the maid looking lost. The bitch opened the door when she saw headlights and stepped out. I waited for her to be gone and followed suit before he woke up. I paid the maid a hundred dollars that was in my pocket and told her to keep her mouth shut. I jogged to my car, went home, and got in my bed like I'd been there all night. She may have fucked him, but my mission was accomplished.

The next day he stopped by to see my daughter and I could tell he was angry but I played off that shit. I told him Brea wanted to go to the park and he had no problem going with us. The next few days, he hung around us but I could tell something was on his mind.

"You ok," I asked him.

"Yup. I'm good."

I saw him looking down at his phone and a grin came across his face. I know this bitch didn't take him back. He got up to leave. Looks like I'm going to have to pay her ass another visit.

Arizona

The shit with Aiden happened two months ago and he was trying his best to show me I could trust him and I'd been trying. Today he wanted to take me to meet his mom and I was a tad bit nervous. He really loved his mom and respected what she thought of any chick he brought home. We pulled up to the house and he told me not to be nervous about anything and that his mom would love me. I'm sure that's what he told all the chicks when they first got there, and then she said hell no. The front door opened and it was an older version of him. He gave me a hug and opened the door wider so I could pass.

"She's pretty, son," I heard him say behind me.

I felt Aiden's hand on my lower back. He guided me to the kitchen where his mom was. When she turned around, I swore I was staring at a young Diahann Carroll. His mom was beautiful, there were no ifs, ands, or butts about it. She smiled and pulled me in for a hug. She smelled just like cake batter.

"Hi, I'm Aiden's mom, but you can call me Daisy."

"Ma, this is Arizona."

"Arizona. That's different, but pretty just like you."

I felt myself blushing.

"Ok bye, Aiden," she said and I looked at him. He put his hands up telling me I was on my own.

"So Arizona, what are your intentions with my son?" Damn, she didn't beat around the bush at all.

"First, can I say I am in love with your son but he doesn't know yet?"

She turned around and put her hand on her hip, "And why haven't you told him?" I didn't want to tell her our business but fuck it.

"Aiden, hurt me in the beginning and I want to make sure that he has my best interest at heart before I allow him in my world. I'm not saying I won't ever tell him, but I also don't want him to play on my feelings. Aiden is all that I see right now. I wake up anticipating talking to and being around him and I go to bed wanting him right next to me. I can see myself having his kids, getting married, and growing old with him. But I have to be sure. I have a lot going on with school and my mom, and I need to know that he'll have my back. Does that make sense to you?" I asked her and she had the biggest smile on her face.

"I think Aiden found himself a winner."

"You think so? I feel like with so much temptation out there, I'm not good enough for him and he'll slip up again."

She dropped the spoon she had in her hand.

"What do you mean again?"

When I told her I think she got madder than I did and I'm the one who walked in on it.

"Listen Arizona, you did the right thing by not allowing him to bully you into being with him. My sons are very arrogant and can intimidate the strongest women you've ever

74

met. If he stayed around and is doing everything to keep you, that means he loves you too. I understand why you're not telling him, but you have to understand he's not telling you, not because he doesn't want you to know, but because he feels like it will scare you away. When my boys love, they love hard, and the only way they'll leave you is if you did something they can't forgive or you end up like the two gold digging hoes they used to be with."

I almost fell out the chair laughing at her.

"What? I call them how I see it. Now, have you and Aiden had sex yet?" I put my head down.

"Don't be ashamed to talk about that. Girl, when a man makes love to you it's a beautiful thing."

"No."

"No what?"

"No, we haven't had sex. I'm still a virgin."

She wiped her hands on her apron and came closer to me. She poured both of us some tea and sat next to me.

"Arizona, you are a beautiful woman and to know you saved yourself for the perfect person makes me see you in a different light. When you choose, choose wisely because, as you know, once it's gone you can't get it back. But take heed to what I'm about to tell you. When you decide to give yourself to a man, to whomever it is, remember what you have in between your legs is a powerful thing. You will be able to get the strongest and most arrogant man to do whatever you want once he tastes that forbidden fruit. The man you give it to will go crazy when he gets it and kill anyone who tries to get it once he's had it."

Shit. She had me nervous as hell. I didn't know if she was speaking about her son, but she had me nervous. Will he really get angry if I gave it to someone else? Am I ready to deal with a man that will be possessive over it? She gave me a lot to think about and until I was sure, Aiden wasn't touching me.

"Baby, you done interrogating her?" His dad said and kissed her neck.

They were lovey dovey most of the night. Now I see why Aiden said he envied his parent's relationship. I wanted what they had too, and I was hoping he was the one, but only time will tell.

"Aiden, I better not find out you cheated on her again," his mom said and he looked at me. We were eating dinner and she just blurted it out.

"Don't look at her like that. She didn't want to tell me. Why would you make her your woman and go cheat on her the same day? That's just fucking stupid."

I was cracking up because then his father started going in on him. He was trying to talk, but his mom was letting him have it.

"I'm going to get your ass later," he whispered in my ear and put his dish away. His mom asked us to stay and watch

76

a movie with her and his dad. I didn't mind because that's probably what we were going to do anyway. Aiden was lying on my lap when the doorbell rang. His dad went to go get it and in walked the bitch from the club. I hopped up so quick, because she deserved a beat down. His mom noticed who it was and rolled her eyes. He sat up on the chair and pulled me back down to sit with him. He had his arms on his legs looking at her.

"I'm sorry to bother you guys but Aiden can I talk to you? It's important."

"Hell no," I said and Aiden snickered.

"Really, Aiden."

"Hell yea, really. You caused enough problems with your hating ass. Whatever you want to tell him you can say it right here. I can guarantee he's going to tell us anyway."

His mom and dad nodded their heads.

"I'm pregnant."

He looked at me and then back at her. He stood up and went to where she was. His hand was around her neck and he had her in the air. I stood there with my arms folded. I could care less if he killed her.

"Is that my baby?"

"Wait, what?" I was shocked that he was asking her that.

"Be quiet, Ari," he yelled back without looking.

"Yes, Aiden. Why would I make that up?"

"How? You were supposed to be on the pill."

"Oh, you're entertaining this? I'm out. Thank you for having me for dinner, Daisy and Block, I really enjoyed myself."

I went to walk by and he grabbed my arm. Was this nigga superman? How the hell did he still have her by the neck and was able to grab me.

"You're not leaving."

"The hell I ain't. This doesn't have shit to do with me."

"What's your name?" I asked her and told him to let go because she was turning blue. When she caught her breath, she told me her name was Cassie.

"Cassie, how far along are you?"

When the bitch said two months my eyes had to grow dark. Aiden shook his head. He couldn't even look me in the face.

"Aiden." He refused to turn around.

"Aiden, look at me," I had tears coming down my face now.

"What Ari?"

"It's over."

"Ari, don't do this."

"You did this to us Aiden. This is all your fault." I started punching him in the chest. He grabbed my arms and tried to hug me but I pushed him back. I could see Cassie staring at us go back and forth.

"YOU COULDN'T KEEP YOUR DICK IN YOUR PANTS AND NOW LOOK. YOU DID THIS."

"It was a mistake. I told you that Ari. Don't leave."

"It was a mistake that you're going to have to deal with forever. I HATE YOU, AIDEN."

"Ari, you don't mean that," he said, looking sad like I hurt his feelings.

"YES I DO. I FUCKIN' HATE YOU. THAT WAS SUPPOSED TO BE ME CARRYING YOUR BABIES, AIDEN. THAT WAS SUPPOSED TO BE ME," I fell against the wall and broke down crying harder. I was in love with this man and now he had a baby on the way.

"Get yourself together, Arizona. I'm going to take you home," his mom said, rubbing my back. I wiped my face and walked over to where Cassie was sitting and kicked that bitch right in her face.

"What the fuck, Ari?" Aiden pushed me back.

"Get the fuck off me. That's for her calling me a bitch. Now that I think of it you slept with her the same night she disrespected me. Damn, Aiden you don't give a fuck about me. You never have. If I weren't scared that you would kill me, I'd spit in your face. You know what, fuck it," I hock spit in his face and shockingly all he did was wipe it off.

"Let's go, Arizona," his mom said when she came back in the room.

79

I cried the whole way to my house. I was hurt, embarrassed, humiliated and most of all sad that I wouldn't be giving him his first child. He took all that away from me because he couldn't keep his dick in his pants. We pulled up to my house and I went to get out, but she stopped me.

"Arizona, I think you handled that pretty well. I couldn't have done it any differently. The spitting was the dramatic exit. I loved it."

I laughed because she didn't care that I spit on her son. I guess she really did like me.

"Arizona, I don't care what he did. I want you to stay in touch with me. I want you to come visit and I promise to make sure he's not around."

I was getting out the car and he was pulling in my driveway. He jumped out the car and came running towards me. I wasn't worried because his mom was there.

"Ari, I'm sorry, don't do this."

"It's over, Aiden. There's no way I can compete with that and I won't."

"I don't want you to compete. I fucked up I know, but we made up and it's all about us."

"No Aiden, it used to be us. Now the two of us just became the four of us. There's not enough room for both of us in your life. I say you choose her because she is the one that's about to give you an heir."

"Ari, I don't care about that. All I care about is you being in my life. Please don't do this."

"Goodbye, Aiden. Daisy, I'll take that into consideration and thanks for the ride."

"Ari, you're not leaving me."

My heart was aching so badly. I stared in his eyes and saw how watery they were. I wanted to keep him in my life and say fuck it, but this wound was too deep.

"I love you, Aiden. I'm so in love with you, but you fucked up. I should've never taken you back. Take care and good luck with the baby."

I went to walk away and I heard a loud crash. I turned around and he'd punched his window out.

"Aiden, calm down," his mom yelled out. He looked at me, jumped back in his car, and sped away.

"I'm sorry, Daisy."

"No, you did what was best for you and not him. He's used to getting what he wants. He has to learn with every action there's a consequence and you were his. He lost a good woman. Don't feel bad for the decision you made. You can call me anytime, even if it's to cry."

She hugged me and got in her car to leave. I opened my door and my sister was sitting on the couch eating ice cream with the television blasting. I doubt if she knew what just happened. She dropped the ice cream when she saw me.

"What's wrong, bookie? What happened?"

I told her what happened and she cried with me. She really grew to love Aiden. Shit, he was at the house so much he basically lived there. I got up took a shower and cried myself to sleep.

Aiden

When Cassie came broadcasting that shit at my mom's house I saw nothing but pain on my girl's face. The part that hurt me the most was her telling me she was supposed to carry my kids and that she hated me. I couldn't function when she said that. It was as if my entire world came crashing down. Watching her cry like that broke my heart. I loved Ari with everything in me and I couldn't even tell her. I was waiting until we got to her house, but it never happened. To hear her say it after she broke up with me had a nigga in his feelings. I felt my eyes getting glossy and had to leave. I wasn't no punk nigga, but crying in front of her and she clearly didn't want to be with me anymore, wasn't an option.

"Yo, what happened?" My brother said when I got to his house. My mom must've told him something because he called my phone and told me to stop by. I started telling him what happened when Farrah came in the room. She was barely dressed. I looked at her then him.

"Don't ask."

"I guess we'll talk later."

"Aiden, you don't have to leave," my brother said, but I was not discussing my business in front of her. Cassie and Farrah weren't the best of friends, but they spoke.

I walked to the door and told Akeem I would see him later. I drove to the ER when I couldn't get the bleeding to stop. Yea, my adrenaline was pumping so much I hadn't even paid attention to how much blood was falling. I sat there for hours waiting for them to stitch me up. I could've gone to our personal doctor, but I wanted to be out my house for a while. They gave me twenty stitches and some pain medication that I popped before I left. I stepped outside and saw Phoenix asking for a wheelchair. The nurse walked back in and asked for a stretcher instead and I watched them bring Ari in.

"What happened to her?" I saw blood coming from the back of her head.

"I don't know. I was in my room and heard a loud noise. I checked her room and she was on the floor. Her body was shaking and foam was coming out her mouth."

The doctors took her to the back and told us to sit in the waiting room. I called my mom and brother. He got there first and I knew it was about to be some shit when his baby mama came in, holding his hand. I don't think Phoenix noticed him right away but I sure as hell saw that smirk Farrah had on her face.

"What happened?"

The minute Phoenix looked up and the both of them locked eyes, I smirked. The look on Farrah's face was priceless. You can see those two had feelings for each other.

"Steel, I'm going to ask you nicely. Please get her out of here," Phoenix said and I guess that's when he realized he was holding her hand, because he let go.

"Phoenix."

"No need to drop her hand because you see me. I don't give a fuck if you're back with her. I just don't see why she's up here."

"I brought her, but we'll go."

"Bye," Phoenix was blunt and to the point with him. They hadn't spoken since the night they slept together. He tried to ask her plenty of times what happened, but she would just say it didn't matter.

"You don't have to say it like that," Farrah should've never opened her mouth.

"Steel, I tried to be nice. Get this bitch the fuck out of here before I beat her ass."

"Calm the fuck down, Phoenix. You ain't about to do shit." I sat back with my arms on the chair. It was about time someone else was in some shit.

"Don't tell me what the fuck to do? That bitch right there is your only concern. I suggest you worry about what the fuck she's doing. Fuck out my face, Steel."

That was it. She pissed him off. I wasn't saying shit. He yoked Phoenix up and whispered something in her ear and made her calm the fuck down. She rolled her eyes and sat back down. What kind of dick control did he have over her ass? I needed to use that on her sister. Steel walked out and came back without Farrah.

"I see you sent her ass home," I said laughing.

"Get the fuck over here, Phoenix."

85

She didn't move.

"NOW."

She stomped towards him and followed him down the hall. I sat there waiting for my mom. The doctor came out and I told him to hold on, I needed to get her sister. I went down the hall and heard moaning. These motherfuckers were in the bathroom fucking.

"Hurry up. The doctor's waiting."

"Shit, Steel. I'm cumming."

I covered my ears and ran away from the door like a kid. I did not want to hear that shit. I told the doctor I would find him when she came back. These niggas didn't come out for another twenty minutes. I shook my head at the perverts and told the nurse to let the doctor know he could come back.

"Hi. Arizona is going to be ok. She suffered a grand mal seizure, which is not uncommon when dealing with stress. Do you know if she's been stressed?" The doctor asked and Phoenix looked at me.

"No. Maybe school."

He nodded his head.

"Ok well she's going to need to be careful with that. Meanwhile, I want her to stay for a few days for observation. If I send her home tonight, she may have another one. I want her to be seizure-free for at least two days before I send her home. Tonight I'm going to run an EEG on her to make sure there's no seizure activity going on in her brain."

"How long is the test?" My brother asked him.

"The test is monitors that are place in her head. They kind of look like heart monitors only they're for the brain. She will need to keep it on for twenty-four hours. This will give us enough time to see if she'll possibly have more or if she's having them and not knowing."

"Thank you," Phoenix said.

We shook the doctor's hand. My mom came running in and asked what happened. Her eyes shot down at me, too.

"Where is she?"

"The doctor said we can see her once she gets in a room."

I had my head in my hands the best I could with this bandage they gave me. I'd really fucked up. I was having a baby by a woman I was no longer with and the one I wanted is so stressed she suffered a seizure. How can my day get any worse?

"What happened to you?" I heard my mom say and I looked up to see Cassie walking in holding her stomach. I didn't move out my seat. I sat my ass right there and let them take her wherever they needed to. I know it's my baby, but right now I was still trying to deny it until it got here. I could feel the stares on me but I gave zero fucks right now.

"Take your ass up there and make sure your baby is fine."

"I don't know if that's my baby."

"Keep telling yourself that. It's not going to get Arizona back," My mom said and pushed me out the seat to stand.

I got up slowly and made my way to the labor and delivery floor. I felt the effects of the pain medicine start kicking in and was going to make this quick. When I walked in her room, she was hooked up to all these machines. I heard this bumping noise echoing throughout the room.

"What's that noise?"

"That's our baby's heartbeat."

I can't front, a small smile crept across my face. I moved back when the doctor came in to take the ultrasound. He showed us what was what on the screen and handed both of us a photo. I put mine in my pocket to show my mom.

My phone started going off. It was a text from Steel telling me they had Ari in a room. I ran out and went to the floor she was on. Phoenix, Steel, and my mom were standing there and stepped out when I came in. She had a bandage wrapped around her head and monitors coming out of it. The doctor said they were doing and EEG so I'm assuming that's what it was. Her eyes started to get glossy when she saw me.

"What do you want, Aiden?"

I sat on the side of her bed and took her hand in mine and kissed it.

"I'm sorry for everything."

She took her hand away and wiped her eyes.

"It's fine. Is that all?"

I could see that same pain that I saw earlier.

"Ari."

"It's Arizona and if there's nothing else, I'm tired. Can you tell everyone they can go home?"

"I love you Arizona and I always will," I kissed her lips and walked out. I heard her screaming and throwing things. I didn't turn around because I felt the tears stinging my own eyes.

"Aiden," I heard my mom calling me but I just kept going.

This was the worst break up I've ever dealt with and I didn't even sniff the pussy. A nigga needed a drink.

Phoenix

When I heard that bang, I got scared as hell. I ran and saw my sister like that and lost it. I was shocked to see Aiden there but I remembered he broke the glass in his car. Steel had the fucking nerve to walk in with his dirty ass baby mama, holding hands at that. She could do all that because truth be told, I was still fucking him and I wasn't stopping. That man had the best dick I ever had and there was no way in hell I was giving that up. The problem I had with him was he thought it was ok for him to sleep with his baby mama but I had to keep my legs closed. I have been, but if I meet someone else he can cancel that shit.

I took my sister home a few days later and the doctor told us if she had another one, most likely she would be placed on medication. He also told her not to stress herself out because it wasn't good for her. I helped her in the bath that she kept saying she wanted to take. There was a knock at the door and it was Steel and Aiden. I moved aside for them to step in. I know Arizona was going to have a fit, but Aiden hasn't been the same since she broke up with him. Steel told me that he barely leaves the house unless it's for emergencies. I told him she was in the bathroom.

"Where you going, nosy?"

"I'm just making sure she's not bugging out," I walked up there and he had her sitting up kissing him.

90

Her arms were wrapped around his neck. I was happy they were making some progress and shut the door. I went back downstairs and Steel wasn't there.

"Come here Phoenix," I heard him calling from my room. My baby had his dick out stroking it and my pussy got wet immediately. I locked the door and turned on the radio. I turned it up pretty loud because he stayed making me scream. I stripped before I got to him and jerked him off, then wrapped my lips around it. I loved sucking my man's dick. Yes, I say my man because neither one of us was going anywhere. I waited for him to cum and swallowed every drop. He told me to sit on his face and when I did this man had me screaming so loud I had to grab one of the pillows.

"I want to feel inside my pussy," he said, pulled me down, and sat me on his giraffe dick. That's what I call it because it's big, thick, and long.

"Phoenix, this shit is so good."

"How good, Steel?"

"Real good, baby."

"Phoenix." I was getting ready to cum. "You know you're pregnant right."

"Oh shit, Steel. Baby, I'm cumming."

He started pounding faster, I guess to cum with me.

"You're having my baby Phoenix. Fuckkkkk. I'm cumming with you."

Shit, we both exploded at the same time. I fell down on his chest to catch my breath. I swore I heard him tell me I was pregnant, but I wasn't about to address it again. I know I better not be. Fuck, now that I think about it we've never used a condom. I sat up and he was staring at me smiling.

"Why are you smiling, weirdo?" I went in the bathroom to get something to wipe us both off.

"You're about to be my baby mama."

"Yea right."

"Yea right my ass. I know my pussy and that one right there is about to bless me with my son."

I laughed at him. He put his clothes on and told me he'll be right back. Twenty minutes later when I stepped out the shower, he came in with a Walgreens bag. He opened up all three boxes and told me to go pee.

"I don't have to go," I lied but I wasn't going in front of him.

"That's fine. I'll wait."

My bladder was filling up quickly and my leg started shaking.

"Get yo' ass in there and pee. Sitting here holding it like a damn kid."

I mushed him in the head and went inside. I went on all three and probably could've gone on more I had so much come out. I came out the bathroom and rolled my eyes at him. He ran

92

in behind me and came out and wrapped his arms around my waist.

"I don't know why you're happy, I'm not keeping it."

He spun me around so fast I got dizzy.

"Don't play with me."

"Steel, I'm already your fucking side chick. Do you want me to have a baby that was made with a woman you're not even with? I'm not being smart when I say this, but isn't that what your dad did to your mom? And here you are telling me to do the same thing."

"Phoenix, the difference is I'm going to be in my kid's life."

I snatched away from him and sat on my bed.

"I don't want a baby like this, Steel. Yes, we should've been more careful, but I don't want it this way." He came and sat next to me on the bed.

"What do you want me to do? She's pregnant, too."

I hopped off my bed. He had his hand going down his face.

"You've been fucking her."

"What do you think?" he had the nerve to say.

"Yo, you and your brother ain't shit."

"Phoenix, stop acting childish. You know what it was when I told you she moved in with me."

"Get the fuck out."

"I ain't going nowhere."

"Nigga, you don't pay any fucking bills here. When I say leave, I mean that shit."

This nigga laid back in the bed like I was playing. I picked my phone up and told her I would see when she got here. I was done with these games he playing. Not too long after I hung the phone up, I heard a horn honking over and over. I glanced out the window and when I heard glass crashing, I laughed.

"Um, that's for you," I pointed out the window.

Farrah was fucking his car up with a steel bat. He went running out there and she started arguing with him. I shut the door and locked it. I went upstairs to check on Arizona and she was asleep under Aiden's arm. I had to wake him up and tell him his brother and girlfriend were outside fighting. He put his shoes on and shook his head, laughing.

"You probably called her."

I smiled and watched him walk out. He stood there watching them, stretching not really caring. Aiden was funny as hell.

"What's going on?" Arizona came downstairs and sat on the couch, looking out the window.

"Nothing. I told his ass to leave and when he didn't, I called his girl to come get him."

"Petty."

"Queen petty, bookie."

The door opened and it was Brian and some guy.

94

"Hey, my boos. What the hell is going on out there?" he said and they both took a seat. Brian had Ari lying on his lap until Aiden came back in the house and cut that shit short. He knew Brian wasn't into my sister, but he didn't want her lying on anyone but him. He was really overprotective of her now.

"Steel wants you Phoenix."

I stepped out the door and noticed it was glass everywhere.

"You think this shit is funny?"

"You should've left when I told you to."

He yanked me up by my arm.

"Phoenix, everything is a fucking game to you. That's why the fuck I can't take you serious. You want to continue fucking a Boss nigga but you can't even be a grown up and deal with shit the right way. You want me to leave her, then make me. Give me a reason besides that baby you're carrying to take me from her."

"If there's a way to take you from her then you shouldn't be with her. You talking about I'm not being a grown up, but who's playing games? I don't have another nigga living with me, fucking him every chance I get. I'm not running to my side nigga's house for some dick. So before you judge me look at yourself. You call yourself a Boss but your bitch ain't in check. Fuck out of here. I don't need you, Steel. Let this be the last time we have sex."

"You mean that."

"Go home to your girl, Steel. You're never going to leave her because she has your daughter. I get it. I'm done with this back and forth with you."

He hopped in Aiden's car and sped off. I didn't care anymore. I was over him screwing both of us and now we're both pregnant. That's bullshit.

Arizona

I was shocked but happy to see Aiden the day I came home from the hospital. I missed him so much that I stressed myself out so badly I ended up having a seizure. Aiden has been here every day since I came home and only leaves if his mom, dad, or brother calls. Today, he was taking me back to his mom's for dinner. I didn't mind but I wanted Phoenix to come and tell Daisy she was pregnant. At first Phoenix wouldn't go, but I talked her into it. Aiden told me to sit in the car while he came around to open the door. He was treating me like I was nine months pregnant or something. He helped me out the car and we all stepped in the house at the same time. His mom and dad gave me a hug and told me to sit on the couch. They didn't want me falling. I told them the doctor said I was fine now and could go back to doing normal things, but nobody listened to me.

Daisy had Phoenix come in the kitchen and I followed, even though Aiden asked me not to. She asked her the same questions she asked me, but the answers were nowhere like the ones I gave. Daisy looked at her and then at me shaking her head.

"What?" I asked and cut open an apple to eat.

"My boys finally met their match. I love it. Block come here," she told him what Phoenix said and he laughed and stepped out.

"Daisy, my sister has something she wants to tell you."

97

She turned around and Phoenix looked at me with an attitude.

"You're pregnant."

"How do you know?" Phoenix asked.

"I see the glow around you."

"Hey Nana," a little girl came running in and then Steel and Farrah walked in behind her.

"How is Nana's baby?"

"I'm fine. Guess what?"

"What?"

"Mommy and daddy said I'm going to be a big sister."

I almost choked on the apple. I looked at my sister and she rolled her eyes and got up to leave. I saw Steel grab her arm and she snatched away from him. Daisy had the evilest look on her face.

"Go see uncle Aiden for a minute, Brea."

"Uncle Aiden, guess what?"

"What?"

She repeated to him what she'd said. I don't know what else was said because I was sitting in here being nosy for my sister. Yup, I sure was. And I was telling her word for word.

"Is that your baby?" she pointed to Farrah's stomach and Farrah looked offended.

"Don't start, ma."

"Akeem, you know I don't like her and she's only with you for your money. I bet she got pregnant on purpose. Didn't you, Farrah?"

When Steel turned his head, she shook her head yes. His mom tried to beat her ass. If it wasn't for Steel jumping in the middle, Daisy would've beat her ass. Aiden came in the kitchen with Block trying to figure out what happened.

"Ma, can we please have one day with you two not arguing?"

"When you stop bringing her ass over here we sure can," she started slamming shit and walked out the kitchen. We all left out behind her and when we walked in the living room, everyone stopped. Brea was lying in Phoenix arms singing nursery rhymes and playing with her hair. I saw nothing but hate in Farrah's eyes.

"Brea, get over here."

"But mommy, I'm singing with Ms. Phoenix."

I left the living room and went to find Daisy. She was in her room lying down on the bed. I got in with her and we both laid there in silence.

"I hate that bitch."

"Why?"

"Arizona, have you ever met someone so vindictive that you see right through them? That's how I am with her. She only wants what Akeem can give her. She doesn't love him and I'm afraid he's going to miss out on finding a good woman to love him the way you love Aiden," she rubbed my face and smiled.

"I know Aiden hurt you, but Arizona he loves the hell out of you."

"I know. I feel the same. I know when I took him back I should've taken into consideration this could happen, but I didn't. I was caught off-guard. I love everything about Aiden, and if that's his baby I will love the baby too. I wish it was me you know?" I wiped my tears.

"I wish it were you too, baby," I turned around and Aiden was leaning on the door.

"Ma, can I talk to Arizona real quick?"

She got up and left us alone. He sat next to me.

"Arizona, I'm sorry for everything that happened. I don't know why I expected you to be ok with it when I don't know if I could if the roles were changed. If you decide you want to be with me, I swear I will drop everything and be the man you need. Arizona, I don't know what you did, but you made me fall in love with you and now I don't see myself without you," he wiped my tears.

"I'm in love with you too, Aiden. I want to still be with you, but I'm scared."

"Don't be scared. After you took me back, I never cheated on you. I'm still that man. I will stay celibate until you're ready. Just tell me you'll still be my girl."

I laughed a little when he said that.

"Don't hurt me, Aiden."

"I won't, baby."

He moved in closer and the kiss was very passionate and sensual. He and I went out hand-in-hand and I saw my sister and his mom smiling.

"Uncle Aiden who is she and why are you holding her hand?"

He got down on his knees.

"Brea, this is Arizona and she is my girlfriend."

"Hi, I'm Brea. Are you the one having my uncle's baby?" I saw Aiden's face get tight.

"It's ok, baby. No, I'm not Brea, but maybe one day."

"Ok. Well when can I come over and play with you and Phoenix?"

"Brea, you're not going over there," Farrah said with venom in her voice. No one answered her. We just pretended she didn't say anything.

After dinner we all went to say goodbye and Daisy gave Phoenix a hug. Farrah was pissed and Steel grabbed Brea and went to the car. I'm sure those two would be arguing later. We drove back to the house and dropped Phoenix off. I promised him I would stay at his house. Again, he helped me out the car, locked up the house, and took me upstairs and ran me a bath.

"You good, baby."

"Aiden. I can take a shower."

"I know but you said this relaxes you a lot."

He picked the rag up and washed my body. He lifted me out the tub, dried me off, and put lotion all over me. His hands were soft and he was gentle touching me. He gave me a shirt to put on and jumped in the shower. He got dressed and got in bed with me. He was watching television while I laid under him, playing a game on my phone. This felt perfect for us. I put my phone on the dresser and told him I was going to sleep. I lifted my head to kiss him and our tongues met. I tossed my leg over his body and got on top of him. I felt his man growing underneath me, but kept kissing him.

I started sucking on his ear, and then I stuck my tongue inside. He let out a low moan and I smiled. I found one of his spots, I guess. I moved down to his neck and I felt his hands moving up and down my body. I sucked on his chest gently and moved further down. I removed his shorts and his man sprung right up. I was nervous as hell but I was going to do what Phoenix told me. I jerked him nice and slow, then wrapped my lips around it and stuck my tongue in the tip. I sucked the head like a lollipop, then opened wide and took him in as much as I could. I felt the spit leaving my mouth, which Phoenix said, was good because men loved that shit.

"Shit, Ari," he was up on his elbows watching. I went down a little lower and sucked on both of his balls and juggled them in my hand at the same time.

"Ahh damn, Ari."

I put him back in my mouth and used both hands to jerk him off and suck at the same time. His dick started twitching, and the next thing I know, I felt something shooting down my throat. I sucked it all out like a pro and I think he loved every minute of it.

"Come here, Ari."

I moved up to him and he pulled me in for a kiss. He flipped me over and removed my shirt and attacked my breasts like they were food. The feeling had me leaking down there. I felt his fingers slide down there and he brought them back up and put them in his mouth.

"I need to taste this right now."

He pushed my legs back and had my clit in his mouth. He sucked on it like he was never going to get it again. His fingers were inside my pussy and my ass. My clit was so hard it felt like it was going to bust and when it did he sucked everything I had out.

"Yes, baby. Suck it just like that."

I felt my hips grinding on his face. A few minutes later I had another one and then another one. He moved back up and I felt the head of his dick at my entrance. I looked down and it was huge and thick. Fuck, was I really ready to do this. He pushed his way in a little at a time but I could tell he was struggling.

"Relax, baby."

I thought about him eating my pussy and found myself relaxing. Once he was in, he stopped.

"Ari, were you a virgin?" I nodded my head. He stared at me and smiled. "Why didn't you tell me?"

"I don't know. Do you like it? Do I make you feel good?" I asked as he stroked in and out, slowly.

"Baby, I can't explain how good it feels. I love it. Shit. Are you ok?"

"Yes, Aiden. At first I wasn't, but now it's so wet I'm enjoying it. Can you fuck me harder?"

Why did I say that? I wasn't ready for that beating. He turned me over and licked my ass and pussy. He entered me again and my body started leaking and I felt that urge to cum again.

"Yea baby, I see it. Cum for me," as soon as he said it, I felt my body shaking.

"Damn, I love the way it looks. Ari, throw your ass back for me."

"Aiden, I don't know how to do that."

He told me what to do and that shit had him exploding.

"Damn, I love you Ari." He fell back on the bed. I used my hands to get him up again. "You sure you can go again?"

"I just want to please you, Aiden."

"Ari, you already did."

"Can you teach me how to ride you?"

He guided me down on his pole and taught me how to do it. I swear a bitch was on cloud nine when I felt it touching my sternum. I enjoyed it more when I stood on my feet. He and I went at it for a while with him teaching me how he liked it.

"Come take a shower with me?" I grabbed his hand in mine.

"Damn, you want some more Ari?" he asked me when I jumped in his arms.

I wanted to not only please him, but also experience everything. I know my pussy was going to be sore as hell for a while, so I may as well try everything now. I never knew a woman or man could cum that many times in a day.

"Ari, I know this may sound cliché, but that's my pussy now. I'll kill anyone that tries to come at you for it."

I smiled listening to him say that. His mom wasn't lying when she said whomever I gave it to would feel like that. That was the main reason I wanted to please him. I wanted him to know how good I was and make him think about what I could give away if it happened again.

"You would kill for me, Aiden?" He lifted my chin up and looked at me.

"I would do anything for you Ari, and if that needs to happen, then yes I would. I love you and I won't allow anyone to hurt you."

"Ok, then."

"I would do anything for you too, Aiden."

"I would never ask you to. I am here to protect you."

"I'll show you I'm your Boss bitch."

"You already have baby."

"I did."

"A Boss bitch is one that can take a little pain and come back with her head held high and you've done that twice already. You already let me know that you'll beat a bitch's ass over me, whether she's pregnant or not. You won't allow anyone to take your spot. You've already proven to me that you don't need me. And you took me back, which was probably the hardest thing you could've ever done."

"Do you want someone to take my spot?"

"Never. No one will ever have me like you do. The baby maybe, but not even Cassie."

"Can I ask you something?"

"Anything, Ari."

"Is that your baby?"

"Ari, I can sit here and lie and tell you no or I'm not sure, but it most likely is. The reason I know this is because when I was messing with her, I always had eyes on her because I was sleeping with her unprotected. But she did tell me she was on the pill. I've been with her for two years and not once did she pop up pregnant. Baby, I hate to say it, but she's probably been planning this for a while. I was always out ripping and running and I wasn't paying her no mind when it came to taking those pills. I didn't even think about it after you took me back. I'm sorry I hurt you."

"I forgive you Aiden, and I promise to try and be there for you when it comes to the baby. I won't treat the baby mean or anything, but I'm not dealing with the kid's mother either. I won't tolerate her disrespecting me and the minute I feel like that's happening and you're not addressing it, I will leave you, quick. Fuck being a Boss bitch, because I'll be a lost bitch and disappear."

"I can respect that. I got you a hundred percent, baby. I love you Ari, and thank you for giving me another chance."

"Who else was I going to get to break my virginity?"

"You saying you used me?"

"Never that. I wanted you to be my first. I wanted to give it to you the night I came there, but other things got in the way. There is no one in this world I would've wanted to have it more than you. I love you so much, Aiden."

I snuggled up under him and went to sleep. I hoped we could stay this happy.

Aiden

I already knew I was in love with Arizona. But now knowing that I was the first to touch her, made me realize there's no other woman out there for me. I'm not saying that because she gave me her most precious gift, because I didn't know. I'm saying that because out of all the women I've been with, she's the only one I'm afraid of losing. Ari let me get to know her mentally before anything physical happened and I was ok with that. I was so into her that I wasn't thinking about anyone. When I lost her, a nigga shut all the way down just like my brother was doing now that Phoenix left him alone.

Today, he and I were finally making our trip to Africa to see what his sperm donor had going on. Yea I call his sperm donor that because my pops is his, and there's no other way to look at it.

"Come here sexy."

I had Ari staying with me now and I loved every minute of waking up to her and going to bed with her. She crawled up to me on the bed and my dick sprung up. She had all types of effects on me. When she saw it pop up, she stopped and let me enjoy the inside of her mouth.

"Mmmmm my man let a lot out today," she said after she finished.

I sat up and put my back to the headboard. I had her turn around and toot her ass in the air, and stuck my face in her pussy. I licked and sucked up and down and had her screaming

108

out when she came. I stuck my finger in her ass, another in her pussy, and sucked her clit until I felt her squirt out. That was the first time I saw her do that.

"What are you doing to me, Aiden?"

She fell back on the bed. I climbed in between her legs and pushed my way in.

"Ahhh, baby."

She always yelled out when I first entered her. I stared in her eyes as I made love to her.

"Arizona."

"Yes, baby. Oh shit, Aiden."

I knew I was hitting her spot because I felt her starting to shake.

"I want you to have my baby."

She opened her eyes and smiled. I saw a tear leaving her face.

"Why are you crying?"

"Baby, I've been waiting for you to ask me."

"Why is that?"

"Because I'm already pregnant."

"You are?" I had a huge smile on my face. I wanted her to finish talking, but both of us were on the verge of cumming.

"Cum on your dick, baby. Show me what you working with."

She started throwing her pussy back under me, which made me thrust harder inside her.

"I'm cumming, Aiden."

"Me too, baby. Ahhh, fuck."

I laid on top of her for a few seconds then jumped off when I remembered her saying she was pregnant. I had her follow me in the bathroom so we could shower together. I washed her body and looked up to catch her crying again.

"Ari, are you going to be a crybaby?" I grinned and stood up.

"I think so. Aiden, I'm so happy that I have you and now you trusted me enough to give me a part of you. I love you so much, baby. Please don't ever leave me."

Damn, everything she said touched me.

"Baby, you're stuck with me for life. I know you can't give me my first, but whatever we have will still be our first together. I love you too, baby."

I kissed her and finished washing us up. I had an hour to get to the strip and board the jet. If I stayed in here any longer, we would be right back at it.

"Aiden, do you have everything. Your toothbrush and all that," she asked coming out the closet dressed in a long dress and sandals. My girl didn't have to be an Instagram model to show how bad she was. Men always think those are the type of women they need on their arm, but Ari showed me it's what's inside that counts. I'm not saying my girl is ugly because that's far from the truth, but it's more to a woman than her looks.

110

"I'm good, baby. Come here," I sat her on my lap.

"Yes."

"I'm going to miss you baby," I told her and she looked like she was about to cry again.

"Don't you dare cry."

She smacked me on my arm and laughed. I lifted her up and we both went downstairs to leave.

"Baby, I'm not staying here while you're gone."

I turned around fast as hell.

"What you mean? This is your house, too."

"I'm not comfortable when you're not here. Plus, you shared this house with plenty of women before me."

"Then look for a new one or have one built, I don't care. But get it done because when I'm out of town you'll be staying in our house. I don't want anyone thinking my girl can't stay home when I'm away."

"I didn't say that for you to tell me to get a new one."

"I know you're not with me for my money Ari, but I want you comfortable when I'm not here. If you're not, then it's my job as your man to fix it."

"Ugh, ok. I guess."

"Where are you staying?"

"With my sister. You know she's five months now. I'm so excited to meet my niece or nephew in a few more months."

"Well, don't go over there crying the entire time."

"Aiden, you're mean."

"I could never be mean to you."

We left the house and she drove with me to the jet and, of course, cried the entire time. My mom told me when women get pregnant, they're very emotional. Well that's what she said when I told her Cassie called me almost every day doing that shit. I haven't told Arizona about that yet, because I know she would flip. She really is riding with me and this pregnancy with another woman. I know it's hard for her and I can see it when I tell her Cassie has an appointment. I fucked up big time, but there's nothing I can do now.

"Aiden, come back to me."

"Arizona I'm only going to be away for two weeks."

"I know, but I haven't been away from you longer than a few hours."

I lifted her chin to look in her eyes.

"You'll be the only person I think about when I'm gone. You know I'm just a phone call away and if you need me I'll jump back on this jet. Ari, take care of my baby," I bent down and kissed her stomach and then back up to do the same to her lips.

"I'll call you when we get there. I love you, baby."

"I love you too, Aiden."

"Alright already. Damn, can we go?" Steel yelled out. He was still salty about the shit with him and Phoenix. "Go get in the car so I can watch you leave."

"But I wanted to see you leave."

"Bye, Ari."

"But..."

"You're such a brat. Get in the car."

She folded her arms and went stomping away. I shook my head, laughing. She was truly indeed spoiled and I wouldn't change it for the world. I stepped on the jet and found a seat by the window. I loved flying, it put me in a zone.

"Ok grouchy. Let's roll," I told Steel and he had the pilot take off.

Steel

I don't know what I was doing taking my ex back. All I know is the night I spent with Phoenix was amazing and when I woke up, she was missing in action. I know it wasn't my sex game, because I put it down in the bedroom. I called her for the next few days, but she wouldn't take my calls. Yea, I could've bombarded my way over there, but I let it be. I was spending more time with my daughter. One thing led to another and I ended up sleeping with Farrah. She started that let's be a family again and I just said fuck it. I moved her and my daughter in. When Phoenix finally did call, it was too late but I still slept with her and never stopped until she put an end to it.

Sitting on this plane listening to my brother talk about how good he and Ari have been lately had me feeling some kind of way. I haven't spoken to Phoenix since the day she had Farrah come to her house, and that was three months ago. I was missing the hell out of her, but I gave her space. My mom has been over there and they been out shopping for a new house and the baby. I told my mom I wanted her in a new place before she gave birth. Farrah was pissed when she found out they were both pregnant at the same time and my mom was catering to her. I don't think she really understood how much my mom hated her. Now that I think about it, she was supposed to be a month behind Phoenix but you couldn't tell. I was definitely questioning her when I got back.

"Go 'head with that shit, Cassie," I heard Aiden yelling

114

in the phone.

"When the baby gets here then I will be, but other than that there's no need for me to come over there."

"What you mean? That's my girl."

"Fuck outta here. Bye, Cassie." He hung the phone up mad as hell.

"What's up, bro?"

"This dumb bitch talking about if I don't come see her when I get back, she's going to make sure I miss the birth. Yo, I'm ready to fuck her up."

I could see the sweat beads pouring down his face.

"Why don't you go see what she wants?"

"Nigga is you crazy. Cassie wants to fuck. That's why she calls every day. I ain't trying to lose Arizona because she wants some dick."

"So tell Arizona."

"Hell no. I'm trying to keep the peace, not create more drama."

We talked a little more in the car that was sent for us and put our game faces on when we got to what I'm assuming was the sperm donor's house. The house was huge, which wasn't unexpected. There were people working outside in the yard and others inside the house. We were escorted to some room that turned out to be a conference area. The table was filled to capacity with guys who appeared to be workers. He went on and on with the introductions and that's when Aiden told him to excuse himself.

"This is my house."

"And this is our business now and if we don't want you here, then it is what it is," Aiden said making me proud.

"You're not my son."

"No, I'm not but that's my brother, like it or not and we running this shit now GET THE FUCK OUT!" Aiden yelled out and Finn and Rowan made sure he found the door.

Yea we brought our own people with us. Once he was out the door, we started the meeting letting anyone know they could leave with no consequences. I'm not trying to work with people who'll try and sabotage shit.

No one left, but as the infamous Miguel Rodriguez once told me. *"Watch everyone when you do a takeover. There will always be someone planning your demise."*

Aiden must've seen what I did because dude was hit right between the eyes. The dude next to him went to say something and he met his demise as well.

"Does anyone else have something to say?" No one said a word.

"Now that the haters are no longer here, our operation should run perfect."

The sperm donor came in yelling about how mad he was I got rid of his longest employees and that let us know right there why they were mad. They probably felt entitled to the spot.

We had been over here for a week so far, and I'm not sure how many people we eliminated for doing dumb shit. Traps were unattended, money was missing, and a bunch of other shit. I told everyone we may have to stay a little longer. We went over every person's background, trying to find someone to run it over here. If we didn't find someone soon I was picking someone from the States. We'd just left a meeting with the sperm donor when I noticed the car going towards the airport where the jet was.

"Where you going?" I asked Aiden, who was getting out the car.

"I don't know about you, but I'm missing my girl."

I glanced out the window and sure enough, his girl stepped off the plane. I put my head down, laughing. She got in the car, followed by someone else.

"Hey Steel," Phoenix said getting in the car. She and I stared at one another before Arizona broke the silence.

"Are you two going to speak or just stare at each other?" I cleared my throat and spoke to her.

"I'm going in my room and well, you know. Don't bother me until tomorrow," he said getting out the car. Phoenix went to get out and I stopped her.

"Have dinner with me."

"I don't know, Steel."

"It's just dinner, Phoenix."

She agreed and we went to this African restaurant and

117

she fell in love with the food right away. Her greedy ass asked to take some back to the hotel.

"I miss you, Phoenix."

"I miss you too Steel, but you know how I feel about your situation. And I'm not changing my mind no matter how much you try and bully me," she told me and smiled. I respected that she didn't want to be that other chick.

"Phoenix, I'm going to make it right."

"I hope so," she stood up and sat on my lap.

"Really?"

"Yes daddy. I've been missing the hell out of that dick."

I moved her back to see her face and she was dead serious. I got our shit and grabbed her hand.

We stepped in my room and wasted no time undressing each other. Neither one of us wanted foreplay at the moment. I slid in her and it felt like home. Her pussy made me let go quickly. I didn't care. She played with her pussy while I stroked my man to get him hard again. We went at it for a while. She and Arizona stayed with us for a week and went back to the States. That was two weeks ago and I sure as hell was happy to be returning home. It took a little longer to get things in order, but we did it. Once a month, one of us will take a trip to check things out. Most of the financial part would be done here. With all the technology out there, everything is possible these days.

I stepped off the plane, and of course Arizona was there

118

waiting for my brother. Waiting with my daughter was Farrah and like I said before, she still didn't look pregnant. Phoenix was six months and she was supposed to be five. I didn't want to cause a scene, so I made a mental note to check that shit out later.

"Go get your girl," Aiden said.

"I will. The minute I get this shit over with."

I'd had a long talk with him, and to be the younger one, he hit me with some things that made me think. Like who would ride for me? What's the real reason behind both of them wanting to be with me? Who am I in love with compared to who I got love for? These were just some of the things I thought about and everything led me back to Phoenix being the one for me.

"Phoenix said to tell you she didn't want to find out what the baby was until you came back. The next doctor's appointment is in two weeks," Arizona told me and gave me a hug.

"Word, Ari. You trying to get with my brother?"

"Never. You're all I see, baby."

"I better be."

"Whatever. Don't nobody want her spoiled ass anyway." She pushed me and swooped her arm in Aiden's.

"I do."

"I know Aiden and that's all that matters. Bye, Hater. I mean, Steel."

I laughed and went in the opposite direction towards my daughter. She came running to me and jumped in my arms.

"How are you, Farrah?" She tried to kiss me and I turned my head.

"What's wrong, Steel?"

"Let's just go home."

I had my daughter in my arms and left her standing there. After we got to the house, I fed my daughter and read her a bedtime story. Farrah came in and rolled her eyes. That's the shit I be talking about. Who the hell is jealous of their daughter? The more I thought about it, the more I know I was about to make the right decision. I hopped in the shower and when I felt the door open, I was happy I just finished taking the soap off. I stepped out and I heard her suck her teeth.

"Really, Steel?"

"Yea. I'm done."

I heard her talking shit. I grabbed some boxers, sweats, and a t-shirt to put on. I grabbed my new Jordan's and my phone. I sent Phoenix a text telling her I was coming over. My mom told me she moved into a five-bedroom min-mansion ten minutes from her. She wanted all her grandkids close and since Aiden and I weren't far, it made sense. She sent me back a naked picture and I felt my dick getting hard. I closed my phone and waited for Farrah to get dressed.

"Sit down, Farrah." She started to put lotion on as I spoke.

"Farrah, I thought we could work it out and get back to where we used to be, but this isn't working."

"Steel, what are you talking about? What happened in Africa because we were doing fine before you left?"

"That's the thing Farrah, we weren't. You saw what you wanted to see. The constant arguing and fighting over dumb shit never stopped and I'm not in love with you anymore. I told you that more than one time, but you insisted it would happen again. Farrah, I'm over this fake relationship and this fake pregnancy you tried to put on me." I didn't know if she was faking or not, but the look on her face let me know I was right.

"Steel, I..."

"What were you thinking, Farrah? Who fakes a fucking pregnancy? If my daughter didn't keep me with you, why would you think a new baby would? My mom was right about you."

"Fuck your mom, Steel. She has never liked me."

"Bitch, if you ever say fuck my mom again I'll kill you." I had her by the neck and against the wall. That was one woman I didn't play around with and she knew that.

I felt her hands reaching out to get me to stop, but I couldn't let her go. It was like I wanted to kill her for driving a wedge between Phoenix and I, all the drama between her and my mom, and this fake pregnancy. I had so much built up and she was feeling my wrath. I watched her turn blue and her eyes were bulging out. My phone ringing pulled me out of the trance and I dropped her body to the floor and left.

"Hey baby. I left the key for you under the rug. I'm going to take a hot bath."

"Ok. I'll be right there." And just like that I was calm again. I hopped in my car and drove over to Phoenix's house. I stepped inside and they did a great job decorating.

I went upstairs after I locked up and went room to room, looking for her. I found the one she occupied because she had the bedroom looking similar to her other one. I saw her laid back in the tub rubbing her stomach, smiling. I stripped and got in with her. I didn't give a fuck that I'd just showered, I needed to feel her close to me.

"I love you Phoenix and I'm sorry for disrespecting you and putting you on the backburner. You didn't deserve that and I understand why you reacted the way you did, but let me make one thing clear."

"What?"

"I let you get away with a lot of shit because I fucked up, but when I tell you something don't make me repeat myself."

"Steel, I just…"

"See, that right there. Shut that shit up and listen to what the fuck I'm saying. You're always trying to get the last word. I'm the fucking BOSS and whatever I say goes."

"I understand Steel, and I'm sorry."

"Then show me just how sorry you are because a nigga not feeling like you are."

She stood up and turned around to straddle me. Once I got hard, she went for her famous ride.

Phoenix

When Steel came over and let me have it, I didn't say shit because he was right. I was always talking shit and trying to get the last word, but I wanted him to understand where I was coming from. I didn't want to be like his mom. I know he has a daughter, but she's lived with him all her life and I know once this baby comes that bitch is going to try everything in her power to keep him away. I put my nightgown on and waited for him to put some boxers and shorts on. I went shopping for him, because I knew when he came back what his plans were.

"Come, Steel," I grabbed his hand and walked him down the hall.

"What's up, Phoenix?"

"Just come on," I had to basically dragging his big ass.

I opened the door and he had a smile on his face. There was a crib, rocking chair, clothes, diapers, and a ton of other things for the baby. I had to wave my hand in front of him just to get his attention. He walked around the room picking things up and grinning. I think him seeing our baby's name across the wall made him happy.

"So you're having my son?"

"Yup. You told me I was that day we found out."

He pulled me in front of him and kissed my neck while rubbing my belly.

"I love you, Phoenix."

"I love you, too."

We were kissing when we heard banging on the front door. He went in the room and grabbed his gun and went to answer it. I saw Aiden come in and say something, but I couldn't hear.

"Get dressed."

I didn't ask questions and did what he said. We pulled up to the hospital and his daughter came running to him. She was crying and the nanny was with her.

"Daddy, mommy got hurt."

"I'm sure she's fine. Let's go see what the doctors are saying."

"What happened, Aiden?" I saw him with his face buried in his phone and I know it wasn't my sister because he told me she was sleep. I swear if he was cheating again we were going to have a problem. Bad enough his baby mama was talking mad shit on social media about Arizona.

"Aiden." He jumped.

"Yea, sis." That's what he started calling me once he and Arizona got back together.

"What happened?"

"Someone strangled Farrah and left her there to die."

"In the house. I'm happy no one hurt Brea."

He gave me this look that verified the answer to my question I was silently asking. He and I walked over to where Steel was with Brea.

"But what about mommy's baby?" Aiden took Brea to the vending machine while the doctor finished talking. I went to go with him, but he grabbed my hand and told me to stay put.

"I checked her mom for the baby that your daughter has been speaking of since she got here."

"Ok."

"Sir, did you know your girlfriend's tubes were tied and burnt. I'm not sure why your daughter assumed she was pregnant, but her mom can never have kids again."

I felt him squeeze the hell out of my hand as I covered my mouth with the other one. His mother was going to flip when she found out Farrah lied. I hoped and prayed I was there when she got her. I know I ain't shit, but she deserved it.

"How is she now?"

"She's stable, but whoever did this crushed her esophagus and her eyes are bleeding a little on the inside."

"That's all they did?" I heard him mumble and I prayed the doctor didn't.

"She should be fine in a few months. If they would have held her a little longer, I'm afraid she wouldn't be here."

"Thanks, doc. We appreciate everything."

"Do you want to go back and see her?"

When Steel said yes and dragged me with him, I was getting nervous. Not from being scared of her, but what he may do to her now that he found out she lied. We stepped in and she had her eyes opened and tubes everywhere. She couldn't speak but by the way she pointed I figured she wanted me to leave.

"Don't move, Phoenix."

I stood there looking around the room, trying not to pay attention. He sat on the edge of the bed and rubbed her face before he grabbed it with his hand and started squeezing it.

"When I leave this hospital, I am taking my daughter with me. I don't want you contacting me or even trying to get in touch with my family to see her. If and when I feel like she wants to see you, I will bring her by. You are lucky my daughter loves you because I should kill you. Not only did you fake a pregnancy, you can't even have kids. This is my only time telling you. If you come anywhere near my daughter, my girl, or my family you'll be dead before you can make it back to your car. Do I make myself clear?" She shook her head yes with tears falling down on her face.

"Good. Now wipe your fucking face and act like you was happy I came to see your trifling ass," he snatched my hand and pulled me out the room.

"Baby, I know you're angry, but can you be careful when you pull me? I am pregnant."

He stopped and stared at me. It was like he wasn't there. A few seconds later, he snapped out of it.

"I'm sorry. I didn't realize I was being rough," he kissed my lips and pulled me closer.

"Brea, will be staying with us until I get us another house."

I nodded my head.

"I'll have new furniture delivered to the house in the morning, but tonight she's going to stay with my mom. Do you have a problem with that?" Like I would say no. This nigga showed me how crazy he was more than once and I'm not trying to get caught up in his wrath.

"Of course. She's a part of you and I have her brother in my stomach. But why do you have to get a new house? I like the one you just brought me."

He smiled, "That's why I love you. You would be fine in a two bedroom."

"If it was just me and my son, of course I would. I don't need all that extra space. I'm only in this big house because your mom threatened me. You know, now I see where you two get your bullying from."

"You know I'm telling her you said that, right."

"You better not or you won't taste this pussy for a while."

"Please, Phoenix. Your entire being belongs to me and I'll take what I want when I want."

"We good?" Aiden said.

"Yea, why what's up?" Steel asked.

"Nothing. I got to make that run we talked about."

"I'll be right back," Steel said and walked off with Aiden. Wherever he was going, he was mad as hell to even make the trip.

"Are we ready?"

"I am. I can't wait to get to Nana's. I just talked to her and she said I could sleep with her and pop pop. I'm going to kick pop pop out the bed, though."

We started cracking up. This was going to be something, but as long as my man got me I'll go for the ride.

The next day, we got up early and went by his mom's house to check on Brea. Steel wanted to sit her down and explain what was going to happen. His mom and I were in the kitchen talking while he tried explaining where her mom was. I know he was mad, but I didn't approve of him keeping her away from Farrah. I would bring it up at a later date, but you can bet I would.

"Hey bookie," I said in the phone when I answered. I noticed Steel's phone rang at the same time. He put it on silent to finish talking. The phone dropped out my hand when she told me what happened.

"What's wrong, Phoenix?"

"I have to get to my sister," I hopped off the island and went running to the car.

"What happened, Phoenix?"

"Where is Aiden?"

"I don't know. Let me call him."

"If my sister has another seizure, I don't know what I would do. She's pregnant and this is too much."

"Phoenix, what's wrong? I can't help you if you don't tell me," Steel said standing in front of me.

"My mom was found dead outside my house."

I sat in the car and it seemed like everyone was talking but I couldn't hear anything leaving their mouths.

Arizona

For the last month, I had been hiding a secret that no one knew. It wasn't a bad one, it was just that I knew my sister would be mad if I told her. When she moved out of our old house I told her to keep it just in case she and I ever wanted to go back, but the truth was my mom had gotten out of rehab and I had her staying there. I went by every day to check on her, make sure she was attending her meetings, and not relapsing. Today I was going by there to talk to her about Aiden. He was the love of my life and I wanted my mom to know she was going to be a grandmother again. She was aware of Phoenix, but I hadn't told her about me yet.

I pulled up at the house and did my normal checking the mail and making sure there were no bottles outside the house. Yes, it's sad, but one can never be too sure. I went to open the door and it looked like the lock was kicked in. It didn't even dawn on me that I didn't have a weapon. I just ran right in. I checked everywhere and didn't see my mom. I went in her room and she was laid back with a single gunshot to the head. My scream was so loud I know someone heard me. I picked my phone up and called the first person I could think of. I called him back-to-back and he didn't answer. I called my sister next and I knew she was on her way.

Someone must've called the cops because I heard them calling out as they entered the house. I could see the sadness in their eyes as I sat there with my moms' head on my lap rocking back and forth. One of the officers called in to dispatch, requesting a coroner. I could hear him telling them to put caution tape around the house and not to allow anyone to pass. I got a text from my sister saying they wouldn't let her pass. I kissed my mom's face and laid her on the bed.

"Oh my God Arizona, are you ok?" I heard Daisy yelling out and embracing me.

"Where's Aiden?" I asked my sister after she hugged me. We looked at Steel and he said he had been calling him, but he was getting his voicemail. Right then, I felt like something was wrong.

"Steel, is he ok?"

"I don't know."

"You don't know. Go find him. Please. I can't take it if something happened to him, too. Steel please just go and find him."

I felt my tears falling faster and I was lightheaded. One of the EMTs must've seen me and came straight over and put the blood pressure cuff on me. Of course it was sky high. They had me sit on the stretcher to calm down.

"Arizona, you have to calm down. You're pregnant and we don't want you to have another seizure," Phoenix said standing next to me.

"I know, but mom is in there and no one can find Aiden. Oh God sis, what if something happens to him?"

"Aiden is probably out handling business," I looked

132

away and wiped my eyes.

"That's not where he is," I thought I mumbled but I guess not. Both Daisy and Phoenix snapped their heads back.

"What do you mean that's not what he's doing?"

"Aiden is cheating on me again."

"WHAT?" I heard both of them say at the same time. I didn't know for sure but I felt it.

"Are you sure? I can't see him cheating after everything you two went through."

"I'm not a hundred percent sure, but I'm definitely ninety-nine."

"What makes you think that?"

"If I tell you guys something, please don't be mad at me."

I saw both of their faces and could tell they wouldn't be.

"What is it, Arizona? If he's doing something how can we be mad at you?"

"He didn't come home last night and this isn't the first time."

"I know you're kidding, right?" his mom said.

"I wish I was. It started happening right before he left for Africa. I smell her on him. I noticed the late night calls. Him saying he had to run out real quick and come back more pissed than when he left. When I asked him if everything was ok, he would just say yes and that was it. He's never stayed away this long, though. He's usually back home by seven or eight, that's why I'm worried. It's after one now and no one has heard from Aiden."

"But I thought when you took him back, you were stuck like glue," Phoenix said, looking upset.

"That was the way he wanted it to look. We would come around you guys and he would shower me with love, but when we left he was out the door. I know it sounds crazy but I'm scared to leave him, and not for fear of my life, but for fear of someone else having him. I can't fathom the thought of another woman being able to call him her man. I love Aiden so much that I'm willing to allow this to go on as long as he comes home."

"Damn," was all Phoenix could say. Oh but his mom called him all kinds of names and couldn't wait to see him. I begged her not to say anything and she promised she wouldn't, but I can't say how long that would last.

"Arizona, are you ok?" I heard Aiden's voice. He came to the stretcher and started hugging me and checking me over. I was pleading with them not to say anything using my eyes. He was kissing all over me and saying how much he loves me and was sorry that he was caught up. Once again, I forgave him just so I knew he wouldn't be with someone else. He stayed with me for the rest of the night and catered to my every need.

The rest of the week flew by and the funeral was sad. We sent my mom off in a gold casket and put a photo album in there with her. The detectives came by a few times, asking if we knew who could want her dead. But she'd been an addict for years so there was no telling. The night of the funeral, Cassie called Aiden's phone and told him she was in labor and that if he didn't want to miss it he had to come now. I didn't know if she was lying or if she really was. All I know is something was going on with him and whether I decide to stay with him or not, I needed to find out.

I made sure I put his iPhone app on his phone so I could track him. Since my mom died, I was paranoid and wanted to make sure he was safe. After everyone left the repast, I put some sneakers, sweats and a sweater on, picked my sister up and went to the address and it damn sure wasn't a hospital. I knocked on the door and the chick that answered smirked, stepped aside, and led me to a bedroom where I found my man lying down watching television naked with just a sheet covering him.

"Aiden, we have company," she said to him. He couldn't see me because she stood in front of me with the door half-closed.

"Who is it?" I saw him stand up and put some shorts on. *Why would he ask who it was? How many people knew about this?*

"Take a guess."

"Stop playing. And why you blocking them."

The moment she moved and he looked in my eyes I

135

saw the fear instantly. He and I stood there, staring each other down in silence. It was then that I heard a baby behind me. I turned around and there she stood with a newborn baby wrapped in a pink blanket.

"Goodbye, Aiden."

He didn't move. I went out to my car, put the key in and sped off. There was nothing I could do. The evidence that I didn't want to see was staring me straight in the face. Aiden was living a double life and no one knew. Well I sure as hell didn't. I know he was a Boss, but this was some serious shit.

"You ok, bookie?" I wiped my eyes, shut my phone off, tossed it out the window, and drove her home.

"Phoenix, you know I love you right."

"Of course."

"Ok. So right now I need to go away. I'll call you soon."

"Don't let him run you away, sis."

"Phoenix, I'm not running. But if I don't get away from him, he's going to cause me another seizure, and possibly a miscarriage. I'm only a few months, but I love my baby and I don't want to risk it."

"Call me as soon as you get to where you are. You know damn well I'm not telling him where you are. I love you, Arizona."

"I love you too, Phoenix."

We exchanged hugs and I rode over to my house to get

some things before I made my exit.

"It's going to be ok," she said and hugged me. I finally broke down and let it all out.

Aiden

The day Ari's mom had her funeral, Cassie called telling me she had the baby which was a lie because she had my daughter two weeks ago. I was pissed because she knew where I was and did the shit on purpose. For the last month or so, she had been telling me she was going to kill herself if I didn't take her back. I told her to go ahead but then I felt like shit when the hospital called and told me she was drinking and driving and got into a car accident. That was right before I went to Africa.

After she left the hospital, she continued with the threats, and since I didn't want her to do it again I started going to her house. At first, I was able to deny all her advances, but one night she had some drinks at her house and I ended up fucking her. Since then, she told me if I didn't play house with her she would tell Arizona. I loved Arizona more than life itself, and I didn't want her hurting again like before, and ending up back in the hospital.

The only people that knew about what was going on was Steel, who I'd just told, and Finn and that's because he and I were messing with cousins. Yes, Cassie's cousin was messing with him and we went out on a few dates. When Cassie said we had company, I figured it was him or Steel. She and I had just finished fucking and I was lying there naked. I threw some clothes on and told her to open the door. When my eyes met Arizona's, my heart dropped. I was busted and there was no getting out of it. I knew Cassie was being smart too when she brought my baby out the room. That was to let Ari know she gave birth and the phone call was a lie.

"Somebody's in trouble," Cassie sat behind me on the bed, taunting me. I sat there in my shorts with my head in my hands, trying to come to grips that I knew I lost Ari for good. I know she wasn't going to take me back after this. She may as well have walked in on us fucking.

"Shut the fuck up, Cassie."

"Don't snap at me. I'm not the one that got caught cheating. Again."

"If you didn't have my daughter in your hands right now, I would choke the fuck out of you." I saw her grip my daughter tighter.

"You got that Cassie."

"What?"

"You didn't have to let her in and see me like that."

"Fuck that, Aiden. I'm tired of you catering to her and forgetting about us. I was here first."

"Catering to her. Cassie, you sound stupid. That was my fucking girl. I'm supposed to cater to her. And what you mean forgetting about you? You are living it up over here and you have an endless bank account, so don't tell me you're not benefitting off me."

"Fuck all that. I want you, too. Why the fuck does she get to have you? I'm the one with your daughter."

"You only have her because you tricked me and stopped taking those pills."

"I've been asking you for a baby since we been together."

"Did it ever occur that I didn't want one with you? You know what? I'm over this shit, Cassie. Don't call me unless something is wrong with my daughter. My mom will contact you when I want her. I can't believe that I fell victim to your ass again."

"You still love me Aiden, that's why."

"Nah, that's far from the truth. Arizona is the only one that can claim my love. I know I lost her after this, but what I'm not going to do is continue fucking you in order to see my daughter. Now you want to kill yourself, go ahead. But I swear if anything happens to my seed while she's in your care, I will kill you and anyone else in your family."

"Really, Aiden?"

"Really, Cassie. I thought I was missing something by not being around my daughter every single day, but men do it all the time and are still constant in the kid's life."

"If you walk out that door Aiden, we won't be here when you come back," she put my daughter down to change her.

"I'll kill you right here if those words leave your mouth again."

"Alright, damn Aiden."

140

I grabbed my shit and ran out her house. I sent a text to Rowan to put a tail on her ass. If that bitch even thought she was going to another town to grocery shop, I wanted to know. I got to my house and it was too late. There was nothing on her side of the closet, her drawers were cleaned out, and her toothbrush was even missing.

"Yo."

"Don't yo me motherfucker. Get your dumb ass to my house right fucking now."

"Ma, it's after midnight."

"Climb up out of that dirty bitch's pussy and get over here."

She hung the phone up in my ear. She must've known what happened because she would never call Ari dirty. I parked in front of her house and saw Ari's car there. I was happy and sad. Happy that I could see her again, but sad because I knew it would be the last time. I dreaded going in the house, but it had to be done. I opened the door and I saw Steel sitting there with Phoenix crying in his arms. My mom was sitting on the couch with her legs out and arms folded and my pops was shaking his head. I looked around and Ari was nowhere to be found.

"I don't know why you're looking for her for, don't you think you fucked her up enough?"

"How could you, Aiden?" Phoenix said.

"I want you to sit here and tell me what that bitch could

141

do for you that Arizona couldn't."

I sat there and told them everything that happened.

"Aiden, my sister had your back through everything. You should've just told her and let her handle it. Now she's gone and no one knows where she is. Believe it or not, she hasn't even called me since she left. What if she has another seizure, Aiden? What if she loses the baby? Did you think about how your actions were going to affect her?"

I listened to Phoenix say that shit to me and she was right. I didn't think about Ari when I was doing my dirt. I assumed Cassie would stop trying to get back with me and everything would be ok.

"FUCK!!!" I yelled out and punched a hole in my mom's wall. She looked at me and rolled her eyes. I grabbed my car keys and left the house. My brother came out behind me and sat in the car with me. He handed me a blunt and a lighter. I needed something to calm me down and this would definitely help.

"Yo, you fucked up bad this time, Aiden," he said and took a pull.

"I know, man. I don't know how I let Cassie knock me off my square like that."

"Yes you do," I looked at him and sucked my teeth.

"She threw the pussy at you and you thought if you gave her the dick, she would keep quiet. But that's not the type of bitch Cassie is. You should've known better being though she trapped you with my niece," he passed the blunt back.

I watched him get out the car and go back in the house. I pulled off and was on my way to my house when my phone rang. I didn't know the number and was hoping it was Ari. The phone dropped and my dumb ass took my eyes off the road for two seconds and hit a damn telephone pole. I don't know how bad the damage was; I could hear people in the background talking. I heard a loud noise and it was them using the Jaws of Life to get me out.

I felt the blood pressure cuff on my arm going by itself. I looked up, and I was in a hospital bed. I thought I was bugging when I saw Arizona sitting in the chair asleep, but it was her. I went to swing my legs off the bed but the machine started beeping and she woke up.

"What are you doing, Aiden? They don't want you out the bed yet."

"Ari, what are you doing here?" I don't know if I was happy or mad.

"I called to tell my sister I made it to where I was safely and she told me about your accident."

"How long have I been here?"

"Two days."

"Two days? It doesn't feel like I was sleep that long."

I went to rub my hand over my head and I felt the bandage. Ari, pressed the button for the nurse to come in. She stood there taking glances every few minutes, but I caught her.

143

The doctor came in and told me I had a concussion and some bruised ribs, but I could go home in a few days.

"Ari, I'm sorry." She put her hand up to tell me to stop talking.

"Aiden, I'm only here because I had to see for myself that you were ok. I don't want to hear any excuses on why you did what you did. All you had to do was trust that I had your back but you didn't, and once again got yourself caught up in the same shit with the same person. Aiden, there's nothing I wouldn't have done for you and I thought you knew that. Can you believe that I knew and I stayed because I refused to allow another woman to call you her man? I was willing to overlook that shit just because I depended on you to love me and never hurt me again. My self-esteem was so fucked up behind you."

"Ari."

"I'm tired of hearing you're sorry. I forgive you and then you do it again. It's clear she has something that I don't. I'm not talking about your daughter, either. I asked you before if you did it because she was better looking or had a better body, and you said no. I knew it wasn't the sex because you hadn't had it yet, but now that you did that must be what it was. She fucked you better than me. She did things for you physically I guess I didn't."

"That wasn't it at all, Ari."

144

"Goodbye, Aiden. I hope the next guy I meet treats me better than you. Maybe my sex will be what he needs and won't cheat."

I felt myself hop off the bed. The blood pressure cuff caught my arm but I snatched that shit and the IV off my arm. I snatched her ass up before she could run out the room and held her against the wall. I could hear the machines going off. I watched the tears roll down her face.

"I told you before not to threaten me but you insist on doing it, so I'm going to say this to you one time and one time only. If you give my pussy away, I will hunt you down and kill you and that motherfucker. If I think you let him taste it, I will kill both of you. Last but not least if, I find out you are even entertaining in another, I will kill him in front of you and then think about keeping you alive."

"Is everything ok in here?" I ignored the nurse.

"Do you understand what the fuck I just said?" She refused to answer.

I told the nurse if she didn't leave the room, she was next. Her ass bounced fast as hell. I wrapped my hand around her hair and took the phone cord from the hospital phone and was about to wrap that shit around her neck.

"Ok Aiden, please. I hear you."

"You hear what, Ari?"

"I better not be with anyone else."

I didn't care that she was crying or shaking. The moment she said she was going to be with someone else, that shit triggered something in my head and I snapped. I stood her up fixed her clothes and got back in the bed.

"Aiden, how are you going to try and tell me...?" I cut her ass off.

"I'm not discussing the shit anymore. You heard what the fuck I said. You can run baby, but you can't hide."

"Why did I ever get involved with you?"

"Too late for regrets now. You got me jumping out my bed because you in here saying some stupid shit. I should fuck you up for that."

"Aiden, this isn't over."

"You're right. You and I will never be over, so get that shit out of your head."

"It's over, Aiden."

"Get the fuck out my room so I can go to sleep. I'm not hearing shit you have to say right now. And I wish you would disappear and see what happens."

She stood there looking stupid.

"Ari, get out my face before I get up again."

She stood there for a few more seconds and then left. I pressed the button for the nurse to come in and give me some pain medication. My body was hurting from yoking her ass up. I sent a message out to one of my other boys to watch her, too. I couldn't risk anything happening to her again.

"How are you feeling?" I sucked my teeth. Her dumb ass is the reason I'm in here. No, she wasn't with me, but if she didn't do that fuck shit of trying to kill herself, I wouldn't be here.

"Where's my daughter?"

"My mom has her. They wouldn't allow kids up here."

"Ok. Then get the fuck out."

"Really, Aiden?"

"Bitch, you thought I was playing when I said don't come around me and only contact me if something is wrong with my daughter."

"Aiden, I know that chick left you by now. We can finally be together."

I rubbed my temples. Why the fuck was everyone testing me today?

"You think because I'm laid up in this hospital I won't fuck you up?"

"Aiden."

"I swear if I had my gun I would blow your fucking brains out. Go, Cassie."

"Aiden, you would kill me."

"Cassie, I lost my fucking girl messing with your stupid ass. If I kill you and go to jail it won't matter because I don't have shit to live for anymore."

"Damn. You are in love with her."

147

"I told you that, you stupid bitch. But you played all these games and I got sucked right in. Cassie, I hate that I ever laid down with you."

"You never loved me like this."

"And I never will. This is my last time telling you to leave before I get up."

I guess she knew I wasn't playing this time because she hauled ass. Now I could finally get some sleep.

Arizona

I talked all that shit to Aiden and even threatened his ass that I was going to fuck someone else, but almost shit myself when he hopped out that fucking bed. I swore he was going to kill me in that hospital room. The nurse just left and didn't even get anyone. Where they do that at? Anyway, when he told me to leave, I went to use the bathroom when I hear that stupid bitch Cassie walk in. I never said he didn't love me, but I didn't know it ran that deep where he felt if I wasn't in his life he had nothing to live for. I wanted to run out the bathroom and tell him all was forgiven, but one, I was scared because he kicked me out, and two, fuck that, he still cheated. But I did follow that bitch Cassie right on out the door. I tapped her on the shoulder, waited for her to turn around, smiled at her and beat that ass. At that moment, nothing mattered to me but fucking her up.

"Yo what you doing?" I felt someone lifting me off her. I turned around and it was Finn. I kicked her in the stomach and ran to my car. I was not about to deal with Aiden again today. The prepaid phone I had rung and it was my sister.

"Girl, are you trying to have that nigga kill you?"

"What are you talking about?" I asked her laughing.

"Bitch, he just called here and said you better be lucky you ran because he was about to fuck you up. What you do now?" I told her what I did and she cussed me out after she laughed. "Girl, I'm starting to think you two idiots belong

149

together. I know he keep doing dumb shit and even though you didn't cheat, you saying and doing shit just as dumb. You better hope nothing is wrong with y'all baby. You know, what never mind. Something is definitely wrong with that baby."

"Oh shit, Phoenix! I'm going to act like you didn't just say that."

"Whatever. Bye bitch, my man wants to fuck."

"Ugh, y'all still fucking with your big ass."

"Don't judge me," she said and hung up.

I parked my truck at Brian's house and walked around the corner to my old house. I had been over here since that shit happened with me catching my ex with his ex. I had finally gotten the blood up and tossed everything from my mom's room. I put a lock on the door. I opened the door to Phoenix's old room, which was across form mine and smiled. Brian and his friend painted it for me two days ago and I had some baby furniture coming tomorrow. I would never keep my son from his father, and now that I decorated both spots, my baby would have his room set up. I was finding out in two weeks what I was having and I couldn't wait.

"GET THE FUCK UP, ARI."

I jumped up out my sleep when I heard his voice. This motherfucker sure didn't lie when he said I couldn't hide.

"I'm tired, Aiden."

I heard him chuckle and got nervous. I turned around and that nigga was pulling my feet to the edge of the bed.

"You think I'm playing with you, Ari."

"Ok Aiden, damn. Where are we going?"

"Home."

"I am home."

"Your home is where the fuck I'm at and this ain't where I'm at."

"Aiden."

"Stop fucking whining and put your shoes on. I'll be waiting in the car."

I stuck my middle finger up at him behind his back. Finn caught me and started cracking up. I thought about running, but most likely he had the place surrounded. I called my sister and she didn't answer. I left her a message that if I came up missing, he did it. I went to make another call and Finn snatched the phone out my hand. I walked out the door with my arms folded and tripped over a rock and almost fell. I saw Aiden laughing his ass off in the car. I was so mad I couldn't do anything but roll my eyes. I closed the door and let my head rest on the seat.

"Get out," I looked and we were at his ex's house.

"You bugging."

He opened the car door from my side and pulled me out.

"Alright, you crazy motherfucker."

"It's about time you realized that. Ring the doorbell."

"Hell no. This your bitch house, you ring it. Wait, don't you have a key?" I was being sarcastic as hell.

"I wasn't going to use it because I figured you would get mad but fuck it."

My mouth hit the floor, "Asshole."

"That's what the fuck you get for being smart. Take your ass in the house," he pushed me in and shut the door. I stood there and he yelled for Cassie to come down the stairs. She had the baby in her hands and he told her to put her in the nursery. She came down the steps giving me a look like she wanted to fight and I was ready.

"I wish you would, Cassie. I'll beat your ass right here."

"Fuck that Aiden, she snuck me at the hospital."

"No she didn't. She whooped your ass, now take that L and shut the hell up."

She did exactly what he said. Now that one was trained.

"Cassie this is Arizona and Arizona this is Cassie. I figured I should introduce you two since you'll be in my life, whether you like it or not."

"She is, but I'm not."

"Ari, shut up."

"Like I was saying, Cassie you have my daughter and the only reason you are to contact me is for that reason only. My mom will be calling you to set up a drop off time for her. There is no need for me to be around you anymore. My girl

152

found out everything, so you can't hold anything over my head anymore. If I find out you fucking with my girl in any way, shape, or form I don't have to tell you what's going to happen."

She rolled her eyes and nodded her head and he pushed me to the door.

"What about her?" she asked, with attitude.

"What about her?"

"You didn't say anything to her."

"And I'm not."

"Why is that? You giving me rules and she gets none."

"Why is that? Maybe, because I hurt her enough so if she wanted to kill you right now, I would let her. Maybe because you knew exactly what you were doing when you stopped taking those pills, or when you opened the door and let her catch me in bed naked. You did so much trying to take me from her and she's still winning."

"I still have your first kid. She'll never get that."

"Maybe not, but she'll always have me and that's what you want the most. You proved that time and time again."

"Fuck you, Aiden."

"No thanks. I'm about to go home and make sweet passionate love to my girl and make her cum until she begs me to stop."

"Aiden, she'll never fuck you like me."

"You're right again. She fucks me way better than you ever did, and that's why she has the key to my heart and will eventually be my wife. Deuces," he chucked up his two fingers, handed her the key and we left. I sat in the car grinning hard as hell. I was psyched that he said I fucked him better than her. That didn't mean he was getting any tonight.

"How did you get out the hospital?"

"Don't worry about all that."

He dropped me off and said he would be back later. I rolled my eyes and went inside and hopped in the shower. I put on one of his shirts and laid down.

"Yes Aiden, just like that," I moaned out when I felt him in between my legs. I put my hand on his head and moved my hips up and down on his face. The second his finger went in my pussy, I came everywhere. My body shook and he thought I was having a seizure. I wrapped my arms around his neck and forced him in. I screamed out and bit down on his shoulder.

"I'm sorry, Ari. I know I keep messing up, but a nigga can't let you go."

"I can't let you go either, Aiden."

"I'm going to be the man you need, Ari. Can you stick it out with me?"

I didn't answer and he put my legs on his shoulders and went deeper.

"Oh God, Aiden. It hurts but it feels so good."

154

"You want me to stop."

"No. Let me get on top."

I got on top and started off slow, before I fucked the shit out of him.

"Aiden, is this my dick?" He grabbed on my hips.

"You know it is." I went up slow and came down hard.

"Oh shit, Ari. What the fuck you doing?"

"You better not give my dick away again." I did the same thing over and over.

"I'm not, Ari. Ahhh shit. You riding the fuck out my dick. I'm about to cum."

"Don't cum yet. I want to suck on my dick."

"Suck all your dick, baby. Yea, just like that. That's your dick Ari, now make me cum."

"Ahhh," he released so much you would think he hadn't had any in a while. I sucked so hard it felt like I sucked all his cum out in one breath.

"Get the fuck up here Ari, and put that pussy on my face."

I did just what he asked and came all over him. He and I went at it for a while until neither one of us could cum anymore.

"That's my dick, Aiden."

"Yea, baby."

"The next time I hear about you fucking someone else, I can guarantee I'll cut it off."

He started choking on the blunt he was smoking. I got up to take a shower, leaving him in his thoughts. He came in behind me and told me I better not threaten him like that because his threats meant more.

"I love you, Arizona."

"I love you too, Aiden."

Phoenix

It seemed like everything was back on track for the moment with Arizona and my relationship. She took Aiden back, which I knew she would. Those two idiots definitely loved each other. Yea, he cheated and threatened to kill her if she moved on, but love makes us do some crazy things. And who am I to judge when I got the crazy nigga's brother in my bed. I gave birth to our son a week ago and it was like Steel or Brea never wanted to leave the house. Both of them wanted to sit up under Akeem Junior all damn day. It was good for me because I could move around and do things. If he cried, his dad could pick him up.

Next week was my sisters' graduation and Aiden set up a surprise party for her. She was seven and a half months pregnant now, and Aiden was spoiling her worse than before. I don't know what he was going to do with two kids and a grown ass spoiled woman. His daughter was so cute, though. Anytime his mom picked her up, Ari would bring her by the house. I'm sure her mom wouldn't be too happy with that, but Aiden put a stop to that shit. I was happy when Ari told me he brought her over there and put her in her place. I wish Steel would do the same with Farrah. That bitch got out the hospital and started making threats because she couldn't see her daughter. Now see, I was going to be nice and allow her to see Brea, but when the bitch said she was going to get Steel back all that went out the window.

"You know I love you, right."

"Yes I do," I turned around and pecked his lips.

"Good, because I want another baby."

"WHAT? Boy, I literally just had him."

"And? I know they say if you have sex right after you deliver you can get pregnant quick."

After he said that I felt his hands pulling my pants down.

"No, Steel. It's too soon to put another one in me." Everything I said fell on deaf ears because my leg was on his shoulder as he feasted.

"Oh shit, Steel. I'm cumming already."

I felt him sucking up all my juices. My clit was still throbbing, and even though I wanted him to stay down there, I needed to feel him inside me. He must've felt the same because in seconds he lifted me up, slid me down, and fucked me against the wall. It always hurt when he first put it in, but once he got me there, the pleasure outweighed the pain.

"Fuck Phoenix, this pussy is going to be the death of me. Fuck me back."

I grabbed onto his neck tighter and went up and down on his dick while he held me.

"Yea baby, just like that."

He laid me on the bed and made me get in all fours. He fucked me so good I went straight to sleep. I woke up naked and he was next to me, watching television with the baby on his chest.

"I tore that ass up."

"Whatever," I stuck my middle finger up at him.

"Thanks for giving me another baby."

"Steel, you don't know that."

"Oh I know. My kids were fighting the entire time until they got to that spot."

"Really. You saw your sperm fighting?"

"No, my dick told me."

"I can't stand you," I was cracking up at the stupid shit he was saying.

I picked my sister up to go shopping for the baby shower that Aiden said she didn't need. He was right because she already had everything for the baby, but it's nothing like having a shower. We were in Macy's when we saw Cassie and Farrah walking around the baby section with Aiden's daughter.

"When the hell did those two start hanging together?" Arizona said, rolling her eyes. I could see her trying to keep her cool but Farrah started cutting the fuck up when she saw me.

"You think because you have his son he won't do the same thing to you he did to me."

"Farrah, what's the real problem? I'm not going to discuss my relationship with you, but if it's something else you want to talk about I'm all ears."

I wasn't about to play these childish games with her. I

159

was still watching Arizona and Cassie out the corner of my eyes. My sister still wanted to whoop her ass, but she promised Aiden no more fighting.

"I think they both are under the assumption that those niggas give a fuck about them," Cassie said picking her baby up out the stroller. That right there told us she was about to talk shit but we couldn't touch her because she was holding the baby.

"I smell jealousy don't you, sis," I said laughing. Farrah stepped in my face and I lost it. This bitch tried coming for me while I had my son. I stepped away from the stroller, grabbed her hair, and snatched her head back.

"Don't do it, Phoenix."

"Mind your business, Arizona," I heard Cassie say behind me.

"Don't ever come for me while I'm with my child. That may be what you do, but not me. I will fuck you up."

"Bitch, get off my hair."

I laughed at her trying to get me to let go.

"Is everything ok?" I heard one of the store clerks say. I released my grip and pushed her away from me.

"Farrah, I got something for that ass." I went to walk to my son and this bitch had the nerve to push me and I fell into his stroller and it fell over. I didn't see anything else after that.

"Oh my God Farrah, her baby," I heard Cassie yell out.

My son started screaming and when I saw the lump

160

forming, I jumped on her faster than white on rice. I slammed her head into the ground and threw punch after punch. The only thing that stopped me was security lifting me up. He pushed me to the back and I saw Farrah jump up and run.

"Get my baby to the hospital, Arizona," I screamed out as they took me to the back. I was pissed when I saw the cops came. They put me in handcuffs and took me down to the station.

"TAKE THOSE FUCKING CUFFS OFF HER NOW!" I heard Steel yelling all the way from the back where I was. He had his mom with him. I'd only been here for twenty minutes and I figured my sister called him and my son was at the hospital.

"Sir, we haven't processed her yet."

"AND YOU WON'T BE CHARGING HER. DON'T MAKE ME TELL YOU TO REMOVE THEM AGAIN."

I glanced over at the officer and he came over and unlocked my wrists. Then I saw another guy come out and his shit read Captain on it.

"Is this your wife, Steel?" he asked and shook his hand.

"Not yet. I want everyone looking for that bitch who put my son in the hospital. How the fuck are they going to arrest my girl when she was protecting our kid?"

"I understand and those officers will be reprimanded. I apologize miss and I hope your baby is ok," he said and his mom rushed me out to the car. *Damn he really is a Boss.*

161

"Is my son ok?" Steel got in the car and I saw nothing but anger in his eyes.

"He's fine, Phoenix. What the fuck was you thinking entertaining Farrah's stupid ass?" *Oh no the fuck he didn't.*

"Steel she…"

"Shut the fuck up, Phoenix. You couldn't walk away?"

"Are you mad that I beat her ass?"

"I don't care if you killed the bitch. What I care about is my son had to get a fucking cat scan and MRI on his head because you couldn't keep it moving."

I couldn't say shit because he was right. I didn't have to go back and forth with her and now my son was in the hospital.

"Take your ass in there and check on my son. Call me the minute they tell you something."

His mom got out the car and went in ahead of me. I felt him yank my neck back.

"If you ever do some stupid shit like that in your life again, my son won't have a mother. Get your stupid ass out my car."

I wanted to cry, but I refused to let him see me like that. I walked in the hospital and the nurse directed me to the pediatric section. I saw Aiden and Arizona standing over his crib. My son had an IV in his arm and the knot on his head was purplish. I ran to him and picked him up and cried.

"Hi, are you mom?" I nodded my head yes.

"Ok. Your son is going to be fine. Luckily, he was strapped in the stroller. It looks to me that he hit his head on the side of that and not the ground. The reason the knot formed is because he's still considered a new born and the impact was hard on his soft head. His CAT scan and MRI were fine and there were no signs of danger in them. I want to keep him overnight for observation, but he can go home first thing in the morning." I wiped my tears and nodded my head.

"It's ok Phoenix," Arizona said and Aiden looked at her. I knew she was about to get it when she got home, too.

"I'll see you tomorrow Phoenix and take care of my nephew," Aiden said and kissed my forehead. I know that was him being smart, but I deserved it.

"Phoenix, I'm not going to lecture you because I'm sure Akeem let you have it some more after I got out the car. I know Farrah is a bitch and I can't stand her, but you cannot allow her to fuck up what you and my son have. She wanted to get under your skin and you let her. Thank goodness nothing was seriously wrong with my grandbaby because you and I would be outside getting it in."

I can't believe his mom just said she would fight me.

"I'm sorry. I would never do anything to hurt my child."

She stood up and rubbed her hand down my face.

"Exactly. But she would."

163

She kissed my cheek and left the room. I thought about what she said and I agreed. Farrah pushed me straight into my son like she wanted him to fall over. I can't wait to see that bitch again.

Steel

I was getting Brea ready to go by my mom's house to go out to eat with my pops. She loved the hell out of my parents and they felt the same. Arizona called me frantically telling me I need to get to the hospital, but wouldn't tell me why. I left Brea with the nanny and called my pops and told him something happened and he had to pick her up. I walked in the emergency room and Aiden was there waiting for me. The receptionist sent us to the back. I saw that knot on his forehead and lost it in the hospital. Arizona told me what happened and I thought about leaving Phoenix's dumb ass in jail for the night, but I know my son would need her being she was breastfeeding him. I understand Farrah pissed her off, but no woman should ever feel the need to fight while her kids are there.

I sent a message to any and every one saying if they see Farrah to bring her to me, dead or alive. I didn't have a clue where she was and I'm usually good at finding people. Wherever she was, it had to be where I would never look. That's ok because Farrah doesn't know how to keep her ass in the house. It was just a matter of time before someone told. I parked in the hospital parking lot and went inside to see my son. Aiden called and told me what the doctor said and that calmed me down a lot. I stepped in the room and Phoenix was on the bed asleep with him next to her. I kissed her forehead and lifted him up and laid him on my chest.

"I'm sorry, Steel," I heard her say just above a whisper. I nodded my head and watched her walk by to use the bathroom. When she came out, she stopped in front of me and pecked my lips. I think she was trying to see if I was still mad.

"He can go home in the morning."

"I know, Aiden called me."

She placed the covers over her and tried to go back to sleep. I looked over at her and smiled. Phoenix may have done some dumb shit, but I know she would never put my son in danger on purpose. I laid him in the crib they had in the room and got in that tight ass bed with her. She moved in closer and I could hear her sniffling.

"Stop crying. He's fine and that's all that matters."

She shook her head and put it on my chest. This chick was going to be my wife and she didn't even know it.

The next day we took him home and Phoenix put him in the bath and fed him. She kept Akeem Junior with her all day in that snuggly thing. I think she was scared to leave him alone and I didn't blame her. A head injury ain't no joke and he's a newborn.

"Daddy, Phoenix won't let me hold the baby," Brea came running in the room with an attitude.

"Brea, the baby was hurt and he wants to be under his mommy. Phoenix will let you hold him when he feels better."

"I want to hold him now," she yelled out. I turned my head and looked at her like she had two heads.

166

"Little girl, take your ass in your room until you calm down."

"No." I snatched her little ass up and put her right in her room.

"Brea, you can come out when you apologize."

"I'm sorry daddy. Can I come out now?" I heard her asking through the door a little while later.

"Are you calm?"

"Yes." I opened the door and she had tears in her eyes.

"Why are you crying, Brea?"

"Because I want to hold my brother."

"And you will, but you have to wait. But when you act like this, you won't hold him. I don't ever want to hear you talking like that again or you will sit in that room until I tell you to come out."

"Ok, daddy." She hugged me and went downstairs.

I'm sure she was acting out because she missed her mom, but I'll be damned if she thinks that talking back is going to fly here. I went back in the room to see what Phoenix was doing and she was crying.

"What's wrong?"

"I should've just let her hold him, but I'm scared."

"Phoenix don't worry about her, she'll be fine. You know she's spoiled and you telling her no is not something she's used to."

"Are you mad I told her no?"

"Phoenix he's your son, too. If you don't want her or anyone to hold him, then don't. I would never get mad over something like that. You're her mom now and she has to respect what you say," I went over and hugged her.

"I'm not trying to replace Farrah."

"I know that baby, but you're the mother figure in her life right now and what you say goes. Her mother may have let her get away with that shit, but it ain't happening over here."

"I love you, Steel."

"I love you, too. You sure you're not pregnant again?"

"Steel, you just came in me yesterday. Shit doesn't happen that fast."

"My sperm is lethal. Your ass steady having crying fits and you cried all the time with him."

She sucked her teeth and mushed me in the head. I kissed her and let her know I was dropping Brea off at my parents and linking up with my brother. He was pissed over what happened at the mall, too.

Aiden

I was fuming when my girl called and told me what happened at the mall. I guess Cassie assumed I was playing when I told her don't say shit to Ari. After I dropped Ari off, I sped over to her house. I know I shouldn't have but there was no way I could allow her to get away with that. And my nephew could've died in the process. I jumped out the car and starting banging on her door. It was a moment like this I wish I didn't give the key back. I heard the doors unlock and the second she opened it I back handed the shit out of her. She tried to run and I caught her by that long ass weave she wore. Now usually I would never put my hands on a woman. My mama raised us better than that, but this situation called for me to.

"I'm sorry, Aiden. I didn't know Farrah was going to do that," I saw the tears coming down her face and had no remorse.

"You out here playing these childish games with my girl, but you had my daughter out there. What you would've done if that was her that hit the floor?" I smacked her ass again and tossed her on the floor where I put my foot on her neck.

"The next time you say anything to my girl or her sister, I'm killing you on sight," I lifted my foot and watched her get up off the ground.

"All this for her, Aiden?"

"This is for my nephew and her. She told me how you

169

approached them, so don't go trying to make this out to be their fault. Then your stupid ass took my daughter out the stroller and continued talking shit because you knew she wouldn't hit you. You put my daughter in danger for no reason, and it better not happen again."

"Fuck you, Aiden." I stepped in her personal space. I put my face close to her neck and listened to her let that soft moan out.

"I know that's what this is all about, but Arizona is the only one that will ever get this dick."

"Get out, Aiden. I hate you."

I laughed at her stupid ass.

"Remember what I said about my daughter. Play with me if you want."

"Kiss my ass, Aiden. She's not even yours."

I stopped in my tracks and turned around to see her with her arms folded, smirking. My daughter was a few months old and she was telling me she wasn't mine.

"What the fuck did you say?"

"Nothing, Aiden."

She tried to close the door, but I put my foot in it and took steps two at a time. I went to each room to find her and she wasn't there.

"Where the fuck is she?"

"Why does it matter? You're about to have a baby with that bitch and she won't exist to you."

170

I smacked her ass across the room and lifted her up by the collar. I dragged her ass out to my car and told her to take me to her. We pulled up to a ranch style house and I snatched her ass out the car.

"Knock on the motherfucking door." She refused to, so I did.

"Who is it?" Someone yelled from behind it. I gave her this look that told her to answer.

"Cassie."

"Bitch, I'm keeping my daughter for the weekend. I told you that."

"Damn no one likes you, huh?"

He opened the door and it was one of the dudes from South Jersey that we had in charge.

"What's up, Aiden? Why is she here with you?"

"Do you want to tell him or do you want me to?"

This bitch broke down crying. He stepped aside so we could come in and my daughter, or his daughter, was in the car seat sucking on her pacifier.

"What are you doing with my daughter?"

"Your daughter? That's my daughter and I got the papers to prove it."

He handed me that shit and I shot Cassie once in the arm and once in the leg.

"Yo, what the fuck?"

"This ain't got shit to do with you, partner."

"What you mean? Come on Aiden, I don't have a problem with you, but you just shot my daughter's mother in my house."

"The bitch should've never lied."

"Lied about what?"

"It doesn't even matter. You should probably get her to the hospital before she bleed out."

I thought about giving the little girl a kiss goodbye but I couldn't force myself to. Finding out she wasn't mine was killing me and as bad as I wanted to kill Cassie, I didn't want the girl to grow up without her. Otherwise that bitch would be stinking. Thinking about all the hurt and pain she inflicted on me and my relationship had me hot to death. I called up Finn and told him to bring me a can of Gasoline. I called up my computer guy and told him to empty that bitch's bank account. When Finn met me at Cassie's house, I poured gasoline all through that bitch and set it on fire. I torched her car right along with it. That bitch won't benefit off me anymore.

I pulled up at my house and Arizona was sitting on the porch in one of the chairs, reading. I sat there, thinking about how she changed my life and how I knew I made the right decision choosing her. I walked up on the steps and put her feet on my lap and laid my head back.

"Baby, you ok?"

That's why I loved her. I didn't say two words and she could tell something was wrong. I saw the anger in her face when I told her what happened. I had to calm her down and keep her from going to the hospital.

"I'm good, Ari. It's better I found out now," I kissed her lips and removed her legs to go in the house. I took my clothes off and jumped in the shower. Something told me she was going to join me and I'm glad she did. I just needed to feel her next to me. Pregnant and all, she washed both of us up, wrapped the towel around herself, and got me ready for bed like I was a kid. She put lotion on me and passed me my clothes. I watched her do the same and get in bed with me.

"Aiden, this is your baby."

I lifted her chin and stared in her eyes.

"I know, baby. I was the first and only one to touch you. There's no doubt in my mind about that baby. It wasn't with her either, but I'm not surprised."

"Huh?"

"I told you in two years that we were together, she never popped up pregnant and then the night she found out I was with you, we slept together. She waited for enough time to pass before she told me. I didn't think it then, but when I look back on a lot of shit, I should've known."

"It's ok, Aiden. I know you loved that little girl. Shit I did, too. It's going to take some time to get over, but you know I got your back."

"You do, huh?"

"Yup. Always even if we're not together," she started

laughing.

"What I tell you about saying that shit, Ari."

"Be quiet Aiden, you know I'm not going anywhere. For some reason, everyone thinks we belong together."

"That's because we do. Now turn over so I can go to sleep."

She backed into me and I lifted her nightgown and pulled my boxers down.

"Aiden, you said you were going to sleep."

"I am. I'm going to sleep in my pussy."

She started cracking up but opened up her legs and gave me her goodies, I know that. The next day she rode with me to my parent's house to tell them what happened and I swore my mom was ready to kill her, too. She went on and on about how she couldn't wait to see her. I came out the bathroom and saw my mom making a plate for Arizona.

"Where's my plate?"

"You aren't pregnant." I sucked my teeth.

"Here baby, you can have some of mine," she fed me some of her pancakes.

"You two make me sick," Phoenix said mushing my head.

"Bro, get your girl. She got a hand problem."

"Only with your ass, she knows I don't play that shit."

"Fine, I'll just take it out on my girl's pussy later."

"Ugh, I can't with y'all." Phoenix got up and left.

"I didn't say anything, Phoenix," Arizona yelled out behind her.

"It doesn't matter; you agree with anything he says."

"She hating baby, give me some more."

We finished eating in the kitchen and left. We went shopping to pick up the stuff she didn't get when they were at the mall. Afterwards, we got some food from the Cheesecake Factory and stayed in for the rest of the night. I wouldn't change any of this for anyone.

Arizona

Today was my graduation day and Aiden was more excited than I was. He woke me up to breakfast in bed and took a shower with me. Of course we had sex in there, but that's nothing new. He pulled a bag out the closet and it was a short coral dress that flared out at the bottom with some strap up sandals to match. The next bag he handed me was from Tiffany's. It was a diamond necklace with my name on it and a bracelet with his name on it. He helped me put both of them on and stood me up in his arms.

"I'm proud of you, baby. You went through a lot of shit and still made it out on top. I love you."

We engaged in a passionate kiss that almost had us late for my graduation.

"Arizona Shevonne Preston."

When he said my name I saw my sister, her man, my man, his parents, and Brea all shouting for me. I was upset my mom couldn't make it, but I knew she was smiling down on me. After the ceremony everyone threw his or her hats up, but I kept mine. I could've tossed mine, but then I wouldn't know which one was mine, and people have bugs.

"Congratulations, auntie."

Yea, Brea started calling me her aunt. I kissed her cheek and put my hat on her head. My sister was doing a great job helping Steel raise her. She wasn't trying to take the place of her mom, but she still had to do what she had to. After everyone congratulated me, Aiden took my hand and sat me in his car. We went out to eat and then over to the club to celebrate. I saw quite a bit of the people I graduated with here. The music was cut off and I was brought on the stage. I saw Aiden get down on one knee and started crying right away.

"Arizona you are nothing less than perfect and I'm happy that you came into my life. Before you, I was reckless and didn't care about anything. It took a while, but you changed me for the better and I will always love you for that. You and I both know God made us for one another, so there's no need to prolong the inevitable. Arizona, will you marry me?"

"Baby, you had me as soon as you got on your knee. Of course I will marry you."

He placed the ring on my finger and we kissed like we were at the altar. He helped me off the stage and that's when I saw Steel go up. Aiden was standing behind me with his chin on my neck.

"Baby is he about..."

He cut me off and told me to listen. When Phoenix stepped on the stage and Steel got down on one knee, she was more hysterical than I was.

"Phoenix, you know you're stuck with me forever, so you may as well marry me." I covered my mouth because I was expecting something nicer.

"Yes, baby."

He lifted her up and kissed her.

"Ok. Looks like the two most eligible bachelors are off the market," the DJ said over the microphone. I saw a few chicks rolling their eyes, but that's all they better do. Aiden was made just for me and no one was taking him from me. Aiden pulled me to the side to talk on the phone with someone.

"Welcome to the family baby girl," his pops said on the phone.

"Thank you."

"We wanted to be there, but someone had to watch the kids and you know my wife is not allowing me in the club with all those honeys alone."

"Give me the phone, Block. Don't get fucked up." I heard him yelling I told you so in the background.

"Congratulations, baby. I told you Aiden loved you. Did you and your sister like the rings? I picked them out."

I put my hand out and stared at the huge yellow pear-shaped diamond that took over my ring finger.

"I love it."

"After the baby shower, you know we're wedding shopping. Wow, I'm going to have two daughters. You just don't know how happy I am," I could hear her sniffling on the phone.

"Awwwww, don't cry. I'm happy that you're going to be my mother-in-law." Aiden saw how watery my eyes were getting and took the phone.

"Bye, mom. You can't have my fiancée crying at her graduation party. Alright, we'll stop by in the morning."

He put the phone in his pocket and walked us upstairs to the VIP area. He had a huge cake up there, some liquor I couldn't drink, and a few gifts. There were some shoes, Celine and Prada bags, and keys to a brand new Lexus truck.

"I love you, Aiden."

"I love you too, baby."

I leaned back and kissed him since I was on his lap. Our section was packed with some of his soldiers and their girlfriends who turned out to be pretty nice but one chick wouldn't stop staring at me.

"I'll be right back baby," he kissed my cheek and got up after someone said something in his ear.

"Can I help you?" I saw Phoenix turn her head.

"No you can't, bitch."

"Bitch. Do I know you?"

"Nah. But your man knows my cousin and they are quite comfortable. I wouldn't get used to the idea of getting married because she's coming back for him."

"Do you hear how stupid you sound? Why would he go through all this to leave me? Matter of fact, who's your cousin?" She stood up and so did Phoenix. Something was going on downstairs but I couldn't worry about that right now.

"Cassie is my cousin." My sister and I busted out laughing.

"The bitch who tried to say my man fathered her baby?"

She returned the laugh this time.

"She may have gotten that one wrong, but the one she's pregnant with now is without a shadow of a doubt his. You see, when he was living that double life fucking both of you, he wasn't smart and ran up in her raw. So guess who's about to be a stepmom?" It was as if all the blood drained from my face. I tried to hide the hurt, but it was evident.

"Bitch, beat it. Even if that is his baby, he doesn't want her," Phoenix said. The bitch went to say something else and gunshots rang out on the dance floor. I froze in place. The shots kept going off and instead of ducking, I stood there looking for Aiden.

"Arizona, get down," Phoenix yelled but I still couldn't move. People were screaming and running and I was walking like a zombie. I couldn't hear anything as I went looking for my fiancé. I got to the bottom step and I heard a familiar voice yelling to get help. Finn, Rowan, and Steel were leaning over someone. They looked up at me.

"Where's Aiden?" I was still unable to see who the person was but I felt it was him. I stopped myself from going any closer.

"Phoenix get her out of here," I heard Steel yelling.

"I'm not leaving until I find Aiden."

"Finn get her out of here."

I saw him coming towards me and I knew something wasn't right. His eyes were glassy and there was blood all over him.

"Is that Aiden?" I was shaking and crying. I could barely see with the tears falling.

"He's going to be fine, Arizona. Let me get you home."

I pushed him out the way and ran over to him. I dropped to the floor not caring that I was pregnant and laid my head in his arms.

"No, Aiden. Wake up, baby. Please wake up. Steel make him get up, please. Come on, baby. We're about to have a baby and get married."

"Watch out everyone. We need to get him to a hospital," I heard the EMT saying but I wouldn't move. I felt a pair of arms around me and I started screaming.

"Get off me. Aiden, wake up. I have to go with him," I started kicking and punching Steel who wouldn't let me go. I tried to get in the ambulance but they wouldn't allow me to do that, either. They closed the back of the ambulance and Steel let me go. I found myself sitting back on the floor crying. I had to be sitting there for a while, because when I looked up no one was there but my sister and me.

"Can you take me to him?" I looked up at Phoenix and she helped me up. There were still a few people outside the club. I was walking by a group of women when I heard that bitch talking to shit.

181

"I guess no one will have him now."

I wiped the tears on my face and stepped back out the car, waddling and everything. I walked up to her and put the gun to the back of her head and emptied the clip in her. I could hear people screaming around me. I saw my sister's face, but she didn't say a word. I put my seatbelt on and told her to drive me to see my man.

Steel

I was standing at the bar when some dude came in looking for my brother. Of course I turned around to see who it was and it was the dude named Jett. He started talking some shit about my brother shooting his baby mother, which I knew all about that shit. Someone must've told Aiden because he came down to where we were. Him and Jett exchanged words and the next thing I know, someone started shooting and Aiden got hit. It wasn't the dude he was arguing with because he was hit, too. Aiden was on the ground with blood pouring out his stomach and all he kept asking for was Arizona. I tried to get him to stop talking, but he wouldn't. When she came over and broke down like that, I think everyone in the club felt bad for her. I saw other chicks crying, Phoenix was stuck, and all I could think about was finding out who had the balls to come in with a gun and let off shots.

I was standing in the emergency room waiting for my mom and pops to get there when I thought I saw Farrah. I wasn't sure so I left it alone and called my fiancé to see if she was on her way. I could tell by the sound of her voice that something else happened after we left. My mom came in and bombarded me with questions because I just told them to get here. Sometimes when you tell people beforehand what's going on, they crash on the way, and I couldn't take that.

"What's up, son?" My pops asked. I didn't know how to tell them my brother might not make it. That's when I saw

Phoenix and Arizona walk in. Arizona was staring off into space and looking straight past us. My mom ran over to her and hugged her tight, and whatever zone she was in it took her out. She started asking for Aiden and that's when my parents looked at me and I still couldn't answer.

"What do you mean is Aiden ok? What happened to him?" My mom asked as she sat next to Arizona.

"Mom, Aiden…" She wouldn't allow me to finish.

"No, no. Don't tell me that. Where is my baby?" She hopped up and went running to the nurse's station, demanding to see him.

"What happened, son?" He sat down next to me and waited for me to speak.

"Pops, someone came in and shot him."

He stood up, stretched his arms out, and walked out the hospital so fast I thought he was jogging. I sat there with my hand on my head. I felt Phoenix rubbing my back and trying to talk to her sister at the same time. Finn and Rowan were both leaned up against the wall. I heard a phone go off and Finn answered it.

"What?"

"Who did it?"

Whatever he just found out he looked over at Arizona and then tried to run up on her. I blocked his path and asked him was he fucking crazy.

"Arizona, did you have to kill her?" I looked at her and she didn't say anything.

"She was pregnant."

I saw her head lean back against the wall. This shit was all the way fucked up. I told Finn he needed to leave and that I would hit him up later. He better hope Aiden doesn't find out he tried to come for his girl because he's not going to live to see another day. The one thing my brother doesn't play about, besides me and my parents, is his girl.

"What the hell happened, Phoenix?"

She told me how the girl was fucking with her inside the club and saying how Aiden got Cassie pregnant for real and she was coming back for him. Then started talking shit about my brother being dead. If you ask me, she got what she deserved then. I know Finn is in his feelings and I understand, but now he's going to have to be watched. I saw Rowan on his phone texting.

"Yo, Rowan."

"I'm already on it. She won't be without escort from here on out. And the video is on its way here."

I nodded my head. It's always good when you have the best working with you. I saw his girlfriend Marcy come in. She gave him a hug and then sat by the girls. They hadn't known each other long, but they were friendly anytime they were around one another. I could tell he was happy it wasn't his chick, but he knew the rules to the game. Rowan and Finn

185

were making major money with us, but they knew what it was that's why I didn't understand why Finn was mad. Yes, she may have been pregnant as he says, but one you couldn't tell, and two he should've told her to keep her mouth shut around Aiden's girl. You don't fuck with a Boss's woman. That's just common sense. That was his mistake.

"How much longer before the doctor comes out?"

We had been up here for five hours and still nothing. My mom was driving the nurses crazy, we didn't know where my pops was, and Arizona was working herself up so much she had to be put in a room and monitored. She still had a little over a month to go with this pregnancy, and we wanted her to wait so my brother could be there.

"The doctor just called and said he'll be down shortly."

My mom started pacing back and forth.

"Can you send him in my daughter-in-law's room?"

The nurse told her yes and we all went in there. Phoenix and Rowan's girl were on both sides of her, watching television. You could hear the news broadcasting what happened inside the club and I guess what Arizona did. Rowan sat down in the chair and had Marcy come sit on his lap and I did the same with Phoenix. My mom ended up lying in the bed with Arizona. We all just sat there in a daze. Someone knocked on the door and walked in.

"Hi, I'm Doctor Patel and I was the one who worked on the guy who I am assuming is your son." My mom shook his hand and wiped her eyes.

"How is he? Is he ok? When can we see him?"

My mom hopped off the bed to throw question after question at him.

"Do you mind if I sit?" My mom waved her hand for him to take a seat. He closed the door before doing so.

"Mrs. Rowan what's your son's name?"

"Aiden Rowan."

"Ok. Mrs. Rowan, your son Aiden was shot four times. Twice in the chest and once in his leg and the other in his hand."

My mom covered her mouth and Arizona sat there looking spaced out again as he spoke.

"We were able to remove the bullets from his hand, leg and one out of his chest. The other one was lodged pretty deep and I was afraid if we tried to get it, we would hit a major artery and he would bleed out. What I want to do, with your permission, is wait a few days to see if by some miracle it will free itself from the tissues it's stuck in."

"Is it going to bother him? Can he move with it there?"

"Right now, he's heavily medicated and asleep. If he goes to move, like I said it may or may not shift. If it does, we can remove it, otherwise we will leave it alone and monitor him every month to make sure there's no change."

187

"When can we see him?"

"Right now he's in the recovery room, but they will be moving him up to ICU shortly. As you know only two visitors at a time in there."

He gave my mom his card and told her he would be in touch.

"Thank God he's going to be ok," my mom said and hugged me tight. Then she went and hugged Arizona who was crying hysterically. Arizona told the nurses she felt fine, and once they realized she was they discharged her. At the same time, they told us we could see Aiden. All of us went to the fourth floor and my mom and I went in first. He had tubes in his nose to help him breathe. There was gauze wrapped around his chest, leg and hand. The IV was dripping some liquid inside and the heart monitors were beeping. He opened his eyes and I could see a few tears coming down. My mom hurried up and wiped them away. Both of us gave him a hug.

"Where is Ari," were the first words he spoke.

"She's fine son. She's in the waiting room right now. Only two of us could come in at a time," my mom told him and kissed all over his face. We stayed in there for about a half hour, then Rowan and his girl went in to see him. We asked Arizona to wait until everyone else went in, because we knew she wasn't going to leave. When Rowan and his girl came out, they said he was demanding to see Arizona. She stood up to go in when a detective and two cops came in.

"Are you the family of Aiden Rowan?" My mom stepped in front of me.

"Yes why?"

"Hi. I'm detective Winder and we're looking for Arizona Preston."

"And why are you looking for her?"

"It's ok, Daisy. You don't have to protect me."

"I'm Arizona Preston. What can I help you with?"

"Arizona Preston, you are under arrest for the murder of Virginia Castle. Anything you say can and will be used against you in the court of law..." as he continued reading her, her rights, the only thing going through my mind was who in the hell was going to tell Aiden.

Aiden

When I got shot, all I could think about was Arizona and my unborn child. The burning was like nothing I'd ever felt before. I could hear her screaming and crying for me to wake up and come back to here, but my body was quickly shutting down. I tried to tell her I was fine, but the words wouldn't come out. I could hear my brother yelling for someone to get her so they could put me on the stretcher. My heart was aching for her because she couldn't take seeing me like that. I would probably be doing the same thing if the roles were reversed. The EMTs cut my shirt open and started sticking a damn IV in my arm. It was like I could hear and feel, but I couldn't respond. I think I coded, because one second I was awake and the next I wasn't.

This last time I opened my eyes, I saw my mom and brother crying over me and that's when I knew I wasn't dead. I couldn't move a lot, but my eyes searched the room and my pops and Arizona were nowhere to be found. But I found out it's because only two people were allowed in the room at a time. My mom told me about Arizona having to be admitted to be monitored due to her working herself up. That only made me want to see her more to show her I was ok. Rowan and his girl came in after my mom and brother left and he told me some other shit went down that we would have to discuss later. We never tried to talk about things in front of our women. The

190

less they knew, the better. Marcy and Arizona had been talking a lot lately, so I know she was hurting for her, too.

They left and I lifted the head part on my bed to see my girl better when she came, but she never did. A half hour passed and still no Arizona. I rang the nurses' station and asked the nurse could she see if my family was still out there. My mom came back in and it looked like she was crying. I didn't say anything and waited for her to tell me what was going on.

"Aiden."

"Yea."

"I have something to tell you about Arizona."

"I hope it's nothing bad because I can't take any bad news," I rested my hand on the side of my legs.

"Umm," I could see her struggling to tell me.

"Spit it out, ma."

"They said Arizona couldn't come in here because she is pregnant. They don't want her to get sick or something like that."

I wanted to say my mom was lying but what she said made a little sense.

"Ok. Tell her to call me."

"Ok. Akeem is on his way to take her home. I'm sure she'll call as soon as she gets home."

She stayed with me all night but I still hadn't seen my dad.

"Where pops?"

"Aiden, I don't think I need to tell you what he's out there doing."

Once she said that I knew he was combing the streets for information. Half these cats didn't know his face, so they wouldn't hesitate to release information to him. I hope he found them soon, because if I did there's nobody that would be able to stop me from taking their lives.

It'd been a week and I was still in ICU and hadn't spoken to my girl yet. Whenever I asked someone where she was, they had an excuse. Rowan came to visit and I used his phone to call her cell and no one answered. I know something was going on but I had no idea what.

"Yo. Why haven't I seen Finn?" I asked and Rowan and my brother looked at one another.

"He's supposed to be my boy and he hasn't brought his ass up here yet."

"Somebody shot Finn's girl and killed her."

"Oh shit. Wasn't that bitch pregnant?"

I didn't mean to sound like I didn't care but I didn't. She was Cassie's cousin and always tried to kick Arizona's back in and I would have to curse her the fuck out. I saw her in VIP the night I got shot. Finn knew I didn't fuck with her like that, nor did I want her anywhere around my girl.

"Damn. She must've pissed somebody off real bad for them to kill her."

"You can say that?" Rowan said, smirking.

"Has anyone found out who shot me?"

"Nah. We keep hearing it was some cats from out of town, but who would dare come in our territory and pull some shit like this? The dude that Cassie had the baby with wasn't even strapped because he knew better. Whoever it was must not know who the fuck we are," my brother said texting away on his phone.

"Yo, what the fuck is going on? Why do I feel like y'all hiding something?" When I said that I felt a sharp pain in my chest and pressed the nurses station.

"Can I help you, Mr. Rowan?"

I saw my brother and Rowan look at me.

"I think I have indigestion or something because my chest is hurting," I told the nurse and a few seconds later I heard the machine was going off and I felt tightness in my chest.

"What the fuck is going on? What's wrong with my brother?" I heard Steel saying, but I didn't know why. I was fine, or so I thought I was, until I heard code blue and them kicking him and Rowan out.

"Mr. Rowan can you hear me?"

Why the fuck were they yelling in my face? I could see the light shining in my eye and sleep was overtaking me.

"Help my brother. Do not let him die," I could hear Steel yelling in the background.

All of a sudden everything went silent and I saw this bright white light. Where the fuck was I and why couldn't I find my brother? This shit was weird. I swore I saw my grandmother and she's dead. Oh shit...

Phoenix

I saw my sister kill a woman in cold blood and she got in the car like nothing happened. I don't know what came over her, but I guess I would react the same if that were Steel. We were all happy that Aiden was alive, but Arizona was now locked up for the murder of Finn's girlfriend and shit wasn't looking good. I sent Steel a message telling him he needed to get down to the station because they were taking her over to the courthouse for a bail hearing. They brought her in a brown outfit that the state gave her. She had handcuffs on and her stomach was showing a little from under her shirt. Her eyes were red and puffy from crying. The lawyer already told us bail will probably be denied, but we were hoping that wasn't the case.

"All rise for Judge Norman Phillips."

We stood up and waited for him to take a seat. He picked up some papers and went through them.

"Judge, on behalf of Arizona Preston we are requesting she be released on bail at this time."

"Your Honor the State is asking for you to deny bail on grounds that she may be a flight risk. Her fiancé has unlimited funds; therefore, we are concerned that he may help her disappear to avoid prosecution."

The judge stared at my sister with the side of his glasses hanging out of his mouth.

"Your Honor, Ms. Preston has never been in trouble with the law and just graduated from college with her Masters in Psychology. She is a law abiding citizen and doesn't pose a flight risk."

The judge banged his gavel down and told both lawyers to be quiet. The doors opened and Rowan and Steel came and sat by Marcy and me. I could see something was wrong in his eyes, but I left it alone for now.

"Ms. Preston, take a step forward please."

The bailiff moved her forward.

"Ms. Preston, you appear to be an intelligent woman, but the decision you made was one of an ignorant person."

"Who the fuck he think he is?" I yelled out and Steel had to cover my mouth.

"Quiet in my courtroom young lady, or you'll be outside."

I rolled my eyes.

"Like I was saying, your decision was a stupid one. You killed a woman in cold blood, then jumped in the car and left. That shows me you had no remorse for what you did, therefore I am denying your bail. You are hereby placed back into the custody of Monmouth County Correctional Facility until your trial, which will be in three to six months."

The judge slammed his gavel down and smirked. I looked at Steel and Rowan who were in there yelling and

Marcy's mouth was on the floor. Something was suspect about this judge.

"How is Aiden? Steel, is he ok," was all she asked as she was walking away. She didn't care that she was going to give birth in jail or that she may spend the rest of her life in there. Aiden was the only thing she thought of. Rowan and Steel both dropped their heads and Arizona passed out. Both of the guys tried to jump over to get to her, but were stopped by some of the court officers. Marcy was rubbing my back as I watched the EMTs put her on a stretcher.

We couldn't even see if she was ok because they wouldn't allow us in the room. Talking about the minute she's discharged, she's going back to jail.

"Baby, how is Aiden?" I heard Marcy ask Rowan. His eyes got glassy and he stood up. Steel had gone back upstairs to check on him after the bail hearing and told us to come up there when we found out what was going on with my sister.

"Aiden umm…" he couldn't even find the words to speak.

"Don't you say that," I told him and he wiped the few tears we saw fall. It was crazy to see the toughest men shed tears for their boy.

"Phoenix, it doesn't look good," he started telling me what happened and how they were kicked out the room. The only reason they came to the courthouse was because his mom and dad were up there and told them they would call when they heard something.

"Oh my God. Arizona is going to go crazy if anything happens to him."

"Yup. But if he makes it, and I know he will because that nigga don't know how to die, he's going to go crazy when he finds out where she is. FUCK! Whoever did this is going to pay dearly," he said, kicking some chairs over.

"What do you mean when he finds out? No one told him yet. It's been a week. He had to be wondering where she was."

"His mom was the one that made that decision not to tell him. She didn't want him trying to leave the hospital, which you know as well as I do he would've. I don't know what your sister did to him, but I've never seen my boy love any woman the way he loves her. The minute he finds out, all hell is going to break loose."

I shook my head because he was right. Aiden was deeply in love with Arizona, and to find out that she was in jail was going to kill him.

"I can't imagine what he's going to do to Finn when he hears that he tried to come for her."

Rowan didn't say anything. He just sat there smirking.

"What's understood doesn't need to be explained," he said and told us he was going to the bathroom.

Marcy and I were sitting in the waiting room when in walked a detective. He came walking straight in our direction.

"Ms. Phoenix Preston, how are you?" *How the hell did he know I was here?*

"How can I help you, detective?" I asked as Rowan was walking over to us.

"I'm looking for the family of Arizona Preston."

One of the doctors came out the back yelling. The detective looked at me like he was confused.

"I'm coming," I stood up and the detective came behind me.

"Really quick Ms. Preston, I just came by to ask you to come down to the station."

"Ok, can I ask what this is about?"

"We have a person of interest in custody that may have been connected to your mothers shooting."

When he said that I started feeling lightheaded. With so much going on, it slipped my mind about asking Steel to look into it.

"Ms. Preston," the doctor said, as I stood there with my mouth hanging open, still in shock from what the detective told me and walked away.

"Yes."

"I need you to come with me right away."

"Is everything ok?"

"It's about your sister and the baby. I'm sorry to tell you this but…"

TO BE CONTINUED…

Made in the USA
Middletown, DE
05 May 2022

65337500R00120